CW00433113

ROSES AND SPINES

NINA DUBEY

Copyright © 2022 by Nina Dubey

All rights reserved.

No portion of this book may be reproduced in any form without written permission from the publisher or author, except as permitted by U.S. copyright law.

CONTENTS

"Is this how you are with your clients? They tell you what to do and you drip all over yourself." I bit my lip and shook my head. It felt so good.

"No, I don't let them-" I gasped as he rubbed a bit faster and I felt myself nearing completion. "I can't-I can't hold it."

"So cum." He purred in that sultry velvet tone...

Chapter One: Mouth Shut

There's nothing glamorous about being a whore. Maybe the job of an escort came with some florid perks but a girl could only be so lucky. There was a fine line that I was quite familiar with at this point, therefore, I wasn't offended.

So when my service was requested, I did exactly what I had been accustom to doing for the past few months. I went into the employee bathroom of Lush, starred at my reflection in the mirror for five minutes while circulating the same four words in my mind: Independent, Safe, Sometimes Smart. It was the only thing that gave my job a purpose. I had to ensure my well being to some extent.

"Rose, wrap it up, you have a client out here waiting for you." I heard my supervisor, Mr. Roth, say in his gravely voice.

I sighed heavily, giving my reflection one last glance before turning to leave the bathroom.

Mr.Roth was exceptionally short and had the worlds farthest receding hairline as a result of poor genetics.

"Sorry, I had to freshen up." I lied.

"Just remember," he began without acknowledging or caring about my time in the bathroom, "no sex. I reminded your guy but you can never be too careful." He said to me as if this were my first week as a Lush girl.

I'd been here for almost 4 months already and though it had been difficult for me in the beginning to understand what this grotesque job entailed, I was no longer considered a novice.

"I know Mr. Roth." I said, approaching the back door of the club. He gave me a nod then walked in the opposite direction as I accosted the gray Benz that would lead me to my fate tonight. • • • • •Steven Greene, or Master as he liked me to call him, brought me to his Upper West Side apartment with that giddy smile he always wore when he requested my services. Even worse, he insisted on awkward small talk at each stop light. I hated small talk with anyone and Steven was no exception even if he was a frequent client that paid me on a consistent basis.

"I had an exhausting day at work." He said, kicking off his shoes once we entered the apartment. "So tease me, play with yourself, and then let me-"

"I got it." I said quickly before the words that followed made me gag.

Lush provided very unique services. Young, conventionally attractive women were employed as shot girls, strippers, or "Lush girls" for the club that serviced men off all ages. The same girls were always up for request meaning, if a man wanted her, he could have her at any time in any place. For a price.

Usually the request was for a simple lap dance or even a strip tease in a private room. However, sex was never an option and the only sexual acts we could undergo was foreplay. Hand jobs, blow jobs, anything involving a dildo, was approved. But of course, there were very specific exceptions.

It was a basic concept but some clients took it to new levels and channeled their inner sadist to enhance their pleasure against the stringent limitations.

Steven Greene was exactly that type of client because he was above the rules. No one could tell him otherwise.

I set my purse down on one of his gaudy pieces of furniture and scanned the room quickly before he came out of his walk-in closet.

Greene had something to prove being nouveau riche in Upper Manhattan with flamboyant art pieces hanging from his walls and golden speckled couch cushions. But above all, he had to prove to me that he exercised control because of all of his money. Which was why I was stuck here with him in the first place and why I would never find what I was looking for.

When I looked back up, Steven was sprawled on his bed with nothing but his reading glasses on. This is what I had to look forward to on a Friday night. A fifty year old realtor with a beer gut and thin strands of brown hair atop his circular head.

"I have a present for you-under here." I said with a smirk, grabbing my crop top from the bottom and slowly lifting it over my head as I swirled my hips to a beat that didn't exist.

"Oh really. Can I help unwrap it?" He winked at me.

"Uh no-Master. I would rather-show you how to unwrap it." I purred, trying hard to keep his hands as far away from my skin as possible.

I tossed the top aside and it landed on a pile of boxes by the wall. Then I ran my hands down my stomach, stopping right at the button of my jeans. I was mildly sad at the fact that they had to be removed from my person since it had taken me a mornings worth of squatting, jumping, and leaning to put them on before work today. I knew they didn't fit but they were my favorite pair of pants and I refused to throw them out.

Wait Rosemary, focus, I had to tell myself when my jeans hit my ankles and I shook them off. Now I stood in a matching violet bra and panty set that made Steven's dick grow. I turned around and bent over to caress my leg and give him a backside view.

"Oh baby, you look amazing." He stated with a moan which was a first since he usually went straight to calling me bitch, slut, and peasant while slapping my thighs with his plastic ruler as if we were doing some type of student-teacher role play. But I expected it soon because like most clients, he could never contain himself for too long.

"You want me to keep unwrapping Master?" I hooked my thumbs into my bra straps.

"Of course you whore." See, there it was. "In fact, do it faster. I want to decorate your stomach tonight." Gross. He was totally serious and shameless. I guess you had to be in order to request this type of service three times a week. It made me wonder when the last time he had sex was. Of course I wouldn't dare ask. We weren't allowed to ask clients personal questions though to me, it would've made the job easier. I'd rather know that my service to one man was the result of him never having touched a woman or simply wanting to try something new for a change. However, other girls at Lush would disagree since knowing less meant feeling less compassion which ultimately meant having peace of mind after it was all said and done.

"Did you hear me?" Steven asked. I returned to the moment I was in and shook my head, unclipping my bra and letting it fall to the ground."I said, sit in the chair for the rest of this." He demanded, wrapping his hand around his member.

I did as I was told and pulled my panties to the side once I was seated. Now I was almost fully exposed to him and he was drinking it all in.

"You like that."

"Yes I do bitch." He growled.

"Does it turn you on when I do this?" I touched my nipple gently with the tip of my finger.

"Oh yeah." He nodded quickly while keeping his dark eyes on me.

"What about this?" I touched between my legs and bit my lip seductively. This seemed to put him closer to the edge and I almost felt sorry that it only took those few gestures to bring him closer to orgasm. Though it was better than my client two nights ago who came at the mere sight of me in a bathrobe.

"Call me Master you slut." Steven said. I gulped at his words but kept that fake seductive expression.

"Look at me Master." I opened my legs wider which caused Steven to moan louder.

"Oh no, I'm gonna cum."

"Please cum."

"Oh you whore. I'm about to-" and right as he was due to say that final word and burst all over his own bed, his bedroom door swung open aggressively revealing two men in black suits. I screamed and fell to the ground, covering myself with my arms.

"What the fuck!"

"Steven Greene, remember us?" One of the men said.

Steven's eyes widened and before he could even respond the men produced two guns and fired directly at my client's naked body.

I instantly started screaming as I used my hands to cover my ears. My eyes were tightly shut as if opening them would make this any worse. I'd never encountered anything like this and a part of me hoped that it was fake but the smarter side of me knew this was very much real.

Seconds later, the only sound that was prevalent was the sound of my shrill screams over a constant ring. I couldn't summon the courage to open my eyes or unplug my ears. However, I eventually did stop screaming since it did nothing to protect me. I was actually alive in this moment.

"I'll finish the girl." I heard one of the men say.

I cowered closer to the wall in fear, wrapping myself in a tighter embrace as if it would make me invisible.

"No need." The other said in a louder tone. "If she's smart she'll keep her mouth shut." He said and I assumed they were both glaring down at my defenseless body.

I shut my eyes tighter and shook my head wanting this all to be a dream. A crazy, sick, realistic dream. But even when I heard the door shut, and I slowly looked up at the damage, I knew this had really happened.

The sheets were freshly stained with vibrant blood as Greene's body lay stiff and lifeless.

My ears rang from the sound of the eight gunshots that murdered Greene. I couldn't wrap my head around any of it because all I knew was that I needed to leave before those men came back. I'd been spared, but that only gave me more of a reason to flee.

CHAPTER TWO: A GUN

I knew that coming into work the next day was a horrible idea, especially considering that the gruesome sight from last night had scarred me and multiple acts of vomiting had led me to feel queasy.

I shouldn't be here. I should be at the police station telling them everything I saw and heard last night. But I was terrified of the warning I'd been given before the men left. I had to keep my mouth shut.

Plus, I'd come up with a story during my cab ride to work. Since everyone knew Steven Greene was my client and they knew I'd been with him last night I would simply say that we were only together for about ten minutes. He relieved himself, paid me, and then I left so I knew nothing about his murder or who murdered him. Crisis averted!

I tried to reassure myself as I straddled the man in front of me in one of the curtain covered lap dance nooks. But it didn't help and within seconds I found myself sprinting out of the nook and darting toward the bathroom.

I gagged into the toilet but nothing came out. Mr. Roth was going to kill me for running out on one of our best customers but I just couldn't center myself and forget about what had happened last night. The images were so vivid in my mind and no matter how much I tried, I couldn't erase the memory.

Sure Steven was an asshole who had given me a fair share of bruises internally and externally from his borderline masochistic desires, but he didn't deserve to die like a scene from The Godfather. Two men with shot guns barging right into his home. It was barbaric.

"Rosemary." I heard a voice call me from outside the door.

I lifted my body up, inhaled deeply, then opened the door to see Charlotte leaned on the wall.

She was a member of the Lush class, an unofficial club for all girls who had been at Lush for a year or longer and had no shame in having sex with clients. There was a mild level of superiority in the Lush class since they claimed the most wealthy clients and they managed some of the "behind the scenes" operations. I had no desire to be in the Lush class and to be honest, if I made it to a year here then I would probably assume that a future for myself was hopeless. More hopeless than I felt it was right now.

"Your guy just stormed out without paying." She pushed off of the wall and blew a strand of red hair from her face. "Said you weren't servicing him properly today."

I moved out of the way for another girl to enter the bathroom then sighed and shook my head.

"Yeah, I wasn't." I walked toward the bar and Charlotte chuckled while following me.

"Are you alright?"

"Uh-yeah, I will be." I lied, reaching over the bar counter to grab a bottle of water.

"If you're off today then just tell Roth. Your attitude is bad for business." She said bluntly. She wasn't being rude, she was being honest and I knew that she was only looking out for me as she always had.

Charlotte was not only the reason why I had a job at Lush. She was also the reason why I had a place to stay in her apartment after I'd been wandering the streets in search of both. I hadn't envisioned myself in an apartment with four others and a job tending to needy men but I was grateful for Charlotte's support and friendship regardless.

"I know, but I'll be fine I'm just a bit tired." I started to walk away but she grabbed my arm and pulled me to a corner by the back hallway.

"Don't bullshit me Rose," she said in a low but intimidating tone.

"I'm not!"

"Oh please, your face is the color of snow and I haven't seen you eat any of the doughnuts in the dressing room that Jade brought this morning." Charlotte pointed out quite humorously. She knew I couldn't resist free sweets of any kind. She'd read me like a book and my heart was racing at the possibility of her knowing something.

"Charlotte, I'm fine."

"You're not! And I don't know if you've heard but your client Greene-"

"Okay yes I saw it!" I blurted out with no control over my words. "Last night I don't know who they are but they came in and shot him and-and-I didn't know what to do." I began to breath rapidly from the memory that I was finally confronting publicly.

"Whoa, what are you talking about?"

"Steven G-Greene-you said something about him."

"Uh yeah, I was going to say that Greene told Roth last night that he would be gone for a few months to avoid some tensions so he left you a check." She rose her brows. "But you're saying he was shot last night?"

I was now speechless. The pressure had gotten to me and I'd done the one thing that I'd been warned not to do.

"No." Was all I could say.

"Yes, Rose you need to call the police and take the rest of today off. This is serious."

"No, I-I have to work." I said, looking past Charlotte at an unattended customer.

"Look I'm not going to tell you what to do and I'm not going to lecture you. But if you saw something then you should say something. If not to the police than to the guys upstairs." She pointed to the stairs down the hallway.

I gave her a blank stare, confused with what I should do next. Why had I opened my mouth? It's not like I was under an obscene amount of pressure. It was just so hard to keep blatant murder a secret when it was consuming my thoughts.

"Anthony just came in, I have to go." Charlotte said, referring to her loyal client that hailed directly from the crime syndicate that had a stronghold on the operations of Lush. She'd been seeing him for a couple of months and he'd already gotten her a new car. The benefits of that Lush class status.

"If you need me for anything just let me know." Charlotte gave me a reassuring smile then made her way across the room to greet Anthony.

• • • • •Maybe I had to tell the police. They'd probably already found the body at this point since I'm sure Steven's neighbors suspected something after last night. I would only be a witness, a job that required me to describe what I saw which wasn't much since the entire time I'd had my eyes closed. I'd barely been able to make out what the two men looked like and I could easily say just that.

Charlotte had suggested I tell the "guys upstairs" but I didn't know any of them the way she knew at least one. I'd never even seen their faces at Lush. All I knew was when they came in, they wore pressed suits and went directly upstairs without being distracted by the naked women around them. Even Anthony only came to see Charlotte on his off days. Otherwise he was right up there with them. Therefore, I didn't see the benefit of going to them with this problem if Greene wasn't directly linked to their pockets.

So I'd come to the conclusion that I would go to police station and explain what had happened. The men who had warned me would never know. How could they?

I pondered this as I waited for my cab later that night outside of the club. I'd worked relatively late tonight since my service wasn't needed outside of Lush tonight. I'd spent the last two hours keeping a married man company and giving a massage to some horny lawyer that smelled of cigar smoke and whiskey.

I glanced down the street to see if my cab was approaching and noticed a black Cadillac pull up a few feet away from where I stood which blocked my line of sight.

The Village was always lively on a Saturday night, but Lush was located on a back street for obvious reasons and this was the ideal time for people to aimlessly roam the streets of New York and come across the hidden gem. I wanted no parts of what happened afterdeck so the urgency to get into a cab tightened at the moment. Especially as one figure came out of the Cadillac and approached me with a slight wave.

"Hi sweetie."He said.

I rolled my eyes assuming this was a typical man in search of some nighttime sexual company. I wasn't in that business so I turned around to go back into Lush but as I pivoted I came in contact with another body directly behind me.

"You can't say 'hi' back?"

"Can I-can I help you?" I cocked my head.

"No, no you can't." The man smirked and then a moment later my head was covered with a sack and my body was hoisted up off the ground and thrown into the back of the Cadillac.

I screamed as I felt my wrists and ankles getting bound together by zip ties.

"You should keep quiet from this point forward unless you want my gun to do the job for you." The man to my right said in an amused tone.

"A gun?" I asked out of fear. I was shaking uncontrollably. I couldn't see a single thing and when I tried to kick my legs up I realized that they bumped the front seat.

"Yes," I felt something poke my side, "a gun." There was a clicking sound and I realized that he'd cocked it right at my rib cage. I was helpless. Who were these people and why did they want me?

I braced myself for the possibility of being raped, murdered, tortured, or all three. What else was I to expect? I couldn't speak because I didn't want a hundred of my skin chunks splattered in this car and these men clearly meant business.

The past two nights had been the worst of my life and I couldn't do anything about it. So I sat quietly, sobbing as the vehicle drove into the night.

CHAPTER THREE: CUTE LITTLE MOUTH

About an hour later, the vehicle slowed and made a sharp turn. A voice in front of me said something in a hushed tone and then the vehicle sped forward, pushing me back a bit on the leather seat.

I didn't want the ride to end. An end to the ride meant the beginning of another mystery and I couldn't bare the thought of what could possibly happen next.

"Carry her inside." The familiar voice that had covered my head said when the vehicle came to a final stop.

"Where am I?" I had to ask out of terror and curiosity.

"Didn't I warn you about keeping your mouth shut?" Whoa, I knew that voice. "If she's smart she'll keep her mouth shut." It was the guy from Greene's house. One of the men who had murdered him! I was going to be murdered!

As my body was lifted out of the seat I began to squirm and scream, making it hard for my captor to secure a grip on me. But man carrying me over his shoulder wasn't fazed enough to release me so I was carried for quite some distance. Down hallways, through doors, and up steps.

"You're as light as a feather sweetie." He said with a chuckle. I didn't let that stop me from squirming and flailing my legs that were bound together. Even if it wasn't causing my captor to let me go, it was at least doing some damage to him. My heels were a modest height but they could be quite painful.

Suddenly, the man carrying me stopped walking and I heard him knock twice on a door.

"Come in." A baritone voice said on the opposite side.

I gasped at the thought of this possibly being my final moment on earth as my body was set in motion once more and I was soon lowered down to the floor. The sack was tugged off of my head. I blinked several times to adjust my eyes to the light and then looked around.

We were in a study. With books on floor to ceiling cherry wood shelves. It had an overall classic but modern look which was odd for a bunch of guys that killed people for a living with me being next on the list.

To my left was a man in a navy blue suit with white streak marks on the jacket and pants. I figured he'd been the one that was carrying me. His brown undercut hairstyle was slightly disheveled as a result of my spastic movement.

To my right was a man with longer brown hair and brown eyes that were focused forward on nothing in particular. Unlike his counterpart, his gray suit was crisp and spotless. Two other men were in the room but they stood by a far wall with stoic expressions.

"I don't know anything." I said, turning to look at the man in the gray suit. "I swear he was just a client. I hated him." Gray Suit exchanged a glance with Navy Suit and smirked condescendingly.

"So did we."

I gulped hard and turned to stare down at my feet. I could see blood from where the zip tie was cutting me and though I wanted to say something, I figured no one would care because why would they. So I closed my eyes to spend my final minute of life in prayer but the very action was cut short by the abrupt sound of the heavy door opening behind us. I sighed as the wood floor echoed with the steps of whomever had entered.

"What's this?" A voice asked. It was the kind of voice that commanded the attention of an entire room without being loud. The kind that held a rich bass undertone but was laced with a sensual velvet ring. If three months at Lush had taught me anything it was the sound and quality of a male voice that could get you in the mood.

"Sorry to disturb you Boss." Gray Suit said.

There was a feeling that engulfed the room as I heard steps near our bodies and as the man they called "Boss" came into my line of sight I had the sudden urge to buckle to my knees and beg for him to show me mercy.

His tall brooding stature was nothing less than intimidating as I turned to follow his movement through the study. Every step he took seemed to imitate my nervous heart beat. What made his presence worse was that the attractive configuration of his features coupled unfairly with his daunting presence.

"This is a Lush girl. She was in the room where we hit Greene." I mashed my lips together while focusing on the "Boss".

"So why is she still alive?" My eyes widened at the honest question he'd just asked. Was it customary to kill a witness? Who was I kidding, of course it was. The rare part of this situation was that I was still alive now.

Blue Suit looked at Gray Suit and held his arms out from his sides.

"See Nate, I told you he'd want the whore dead."

"I'm not a whore." I muttered the false statement. Of course I was a whore but they'd degraded me so much prior to this moment that I needed control over something. That something was my identity.

Everyone looked at me after I dared to speak. The Boss nodded then leaned back against the large wood desk and put his hands in his pockets casually.

"Has she been feisty the whole time?"

"Yeah, she's a feisty one." Blue Suit said, pointing to his attire which amused me quite a bit. "She's also not one for following directions." The Boss narrowed his eyes.

"How much did she see?"

"Enough," Nate began, "She chronicled the entire thing to Charlotte."

"Who?"

"Anthony's girl."

Had Charlotte told them? She'd mentioned bringing the issue to the "guys upstairs", maybe they were those guys. Either way I felt betrayed regardless of her intentions. Malicious or not, that possibly got me into this situation. This horrible situation where I was scared, in pain, and blind to what was to become of my future.

"I-I didn't say anything to her that wasn't true." I protested, wincing from the pain on my ankles. "He was shot and I couldn't just-"

"I'm gonna make myself very clear you whore."

"I'm not a-"

"Be quiet." The Boss interrupted in the same calm tone that he'd entered the room with.

He pushed off of the desk and approached me slowly. "You're a very lucky girl. Steven Greene was a snake and you made the mistake of opening that cute little mouth of yours today." He looked at my lips then his eyes traveled down to my feet. "So you're staying here and if you so much as breath with that attitude then you'll be in the same condition as your fat, dirty client." He stared into my eyes, "Understand?"

I buckled back at his threat and shivered at his mere presence before me. I gave him a timid nod to show that I understood.

"Where do we put her Boss?" Nate asked.

The Boss' eyes scanned my body once more then our eyes met and for a second I thought I could guilt him into having pity on me. But the moment ended as quick as it began when he said,

"The basement." Then he walked away, exiting the study.

I was going to a basement to suffer. How long would I be here? I was starting to whole heartedly regret my choice to open my "cute" mouth at Lush this morning. Simply put, the men in the room were right, I was a whore. A stupid whore.

CHAPTER FOUR: THE BOSS

I had just turned twenty-one when it all happened. Getting evicted or kicked out of apartment after apartment had really taken its toll and I shivered on the front steps of what seemed to be a post office after a full day of roaming the busy streets.

There were no other people on the streets but at a distance I could hear the faint sound of police sirens and the thumping of a heavy bass beat.

I didn't know where to go. I only knew one other person in New York and that was Rebecca Santana from my last job as a waitress. She'd been the only employee to warn me about the harsh reality of working late shifts at the diner where drunk men were daring and perverted. Though, despite her words, I'd evidently ended up kicking a customer who purposely grazed my ass as I brought over a steaming bowl of soup. But the tip of the ice berg, and the act that had gotten me fired, was my poor decision to slap the cheek of a mafia man after he grabbed my chest. Immediately after I did it I knew I was in trouble regardless of how violated I felt from his actions.

Rebecca gave me her phone number when I left, in case of an emergency. She knew of my hopeless situation and she knew I had nowhere to go.

But should I call her? It had been a few days since I'd been fired and I was sure that she was busy. She was a single mother and the last thing she needed was my grown ass squatting on her sofa for several nights job searching while eating ramen noodles.

I stood up, grabbed my duffle and headed down the street. I didn't know where I was going, but I figured walking toward the sound was my best gamble. • • • • • •There was a hard knock on the door that sat at the top of the staircase. The staircase led down to the dingy basement that I'd spent the entire night in. I hadn't slept, partially because the twin sized bed by the far wall looked as if it were rusting to the point of no return. The other reason was because I had been kidnapped and I didn't feel that closing my eyes was an appropriate thing to do.

It wasn't a large space but I was sure that the door by the stereo set led to a more lavish area that was unfortunately locked. They'd shoved me in this antique room with a non functioning kitchenette and two windows that were too small for even a mouse to crawl through.

The knock sounded again but this time it was followed by a voice.

"Can I come down?" I wasn't familiar with the soft voice that spoke but I simply responded with a "yes" and heard footsteps descending to my jail.

"Good morning." A blonde haired woman who wore a white body con dress and navy blue heels approached me with a tray in her hand. "I have your breakfast."

My expression was that of confusion as I sat on a wooden chair. The same chair I had sat on all night.

"I'm not hungry." I lied but only because I refused to believe anyone cared enough to feed me. I'd gone two days without food before. This was nothing.

"Oh," she paused and pressed her lips together. "I was told to bring food to you."

"They care enough to feed me here?" I found that highly unlikely.

The woman sighed and set the tray down on the table in front of me.

"Right." She gave me an apologetic look. "I'm sorry-uh-I don't recall your name."

"Rosemary." She repeated my name silently then smiled.

"I'm Hannah. I'll be bringing your meals down for-" she paused and shook her head. "I'll be sure to make this situation a bit more accommodating for you Rosemary."

"Really?" Her face said it all by the unsure expression.

"I'll try my best." She assured but I still knew her best wasn't possible. I was stuck here.

I nodded then looked down at the stack of pancakes, turkey bacon strips, strawberries, and glass of orange juice on the tray. It looked and smelled amazing.

"When can I leave?" I utilized her compassion to find an answer for this lingering question that pegged me.

"I'm sorry but I don't have that information." She smiled apologetically. She was only here to do the bare minimum for me and had little control. Just like a shot girl as Lush.

"Good morning." Nate appeared on the stairs in slacks and a button down. I hadn't even heard the door close. At least Hannah had the courtesy to knock.

"Aw, Hannah made a friend." Blue Suit, aka the man who had carried me last night from the car, appeared behind Nate in the exact suit he had worn last night. Apparently someone had spent the night murdering more innocent people and didn't have time to change. Or so I believed.

"Why're you guys down here?" Hannah asked out of curiosity.

"We're here to help." Blue Suit said.

"I got it Lance. Shouldn't you wash up? You had a long night."

"There's been a change of plans." Lance said, ignoring Hannah's suggestion. "Donovan wants the girl taken to see Robert."

"Rosemary?" Hannah asked in reference to Lance referring to me as "the girl".

"Innocent name." Nate complimented with a smirk then nodded. "So we'll take it from here."

Hannah looked at me with compassionate eyes. I'd been quiet the entire time but simply being the prisoner of the day drew enough attention to me. Hannah had given me only a minute of hope but now I was in the hands of criminal monsters and I had to follow them up.

Robert was actually Dr. Robert Thornton, the in house physician. He occupied an office space just above the basement in what I was now realizing was a huge mansion consisting of a vast number of staff that questioned nothing.

Dr. Thornton examined my scarred ankles and treated them with ointment before wrapping each in a bandage.

"Do you feel light headed?" I knew what he meant to ask. Did the murder leave me feeling that way? But he wouldn't say it that blatantly. I was exceptional at reading into people since Lush was a haven for men to rely on the girls to know what they wanted and needed. It could easily be considered an art.

"I do." I responded quickly, but thought before I continued. "I've never seen a person die before." I should've said murdered but I had to tread lightly. So I sighed, hearing the gunshots play again in my head.

The doctor scribbled something down in a folder. Did he care at all? I doubted it. He just wanted me out of his exam room. But I needed to at least try.

"I'll be sure to notify Donovan."

"Who?"

"The boss." Dr. Thornton closed the folder and clicked his pen.

"But-he already knows." That's why I was here!

"I'll give you some medication if you believe that will help your-"

"No! I mean-no thank you. I would just like to go home."

"Hey doc," I heard Nate call outside the door. "Is she good to go?"

"Yes, she's all clear." The doctor opened the door but I didn't move. Although this entire house was my prison, this particular spot felt safe. As if anyone who was not a doctor couldn't step foot near me.

But my vision was crushed when I saw a pair of cuffs dangling from Nate's pocket. He was leaned against the wall and when he noticed that I wasn't in motion he followed my gaze.

"Don't make me use these." I looked at Dr. Thornton who was outstandingly useless as he simply sat behind a computer screen and avoided my eyes completely.

I got off of the table and went out into the hallway with Nate and Lance who prompted me to follow alongside them. At this rate I just wanted to be alive and not bound like cattle.

As we ventured further, I was truly able to see the various features of the mansion. It was all relatively modern with floors lined in dark bamboo wood and walls that adorned a rich creamy white color. What surprised me most was the art work that lined the walls and the few sculptural pieces in the halls. A set of grand satires led to the second level which kept the same themes but included more doorways.

Everything about this place screamed elegance and wealth in a way that non of my experiences would be able to compare to. I wasn't sure if this was a home or a place of work. It seemed to be something of a hybrid, like one of those high end safe houses in a spy movie.

"I feel like a damn babysitter today." I heard Lance say in a bit of a hushed tone.

"Yeah, well at least she's cute." Nate said.

If it weren't for the fact that these men had kidnapped me and stuck me in a basement then I would actually be appreciative to have them be Lush clients of mine. Handsome, charming, and strong would have been a nice change of pace at Lush. Not to mention, they knew what they were doing with bondage material.

But since I currently hated everyone in this situation, it was easy to ignore their aesthetic appeal. Especially as Lance knocked on a large wooden door which would reveal the real test of my ability to ignore aesthetic appeal.

There was no response but Lance opened the door and Nate nudged me inside the same study I'd been in last night.

By the fireplace, the Boss was talking to Hannah who was pointing to something on her iPad screen. However, when we stepped further into the study, he looked up and furrowed his eyebrows in confusion.

"What happened to you?" The Boss asked, looking directly at Lance.

Lance shifted uncomfortably, knowing that his suit was a mess. Maybe he hadn't spent the night murdering more people since he was so awkward about a simple question.

"I ran into some trouble after everything last night." He cleared his throat as Nate chuckled softly.

"Trouble is an understatement." Hannah said. "He had a four hour walk back here after messing with the wrong girl."

Even I was tempted to laugh at that, considering it karma for how they treated me last night. Now I needed the same thing to happen to Nate and then I'd have peace of mind before they all killed me.

The Boss didn't further entertain this, he simply sighed and looked at Hannah.

"Give us a moment." He then nodded to Lance and Nate.

They all filed out of the study and it took me a moment to realize that it was just the two of us which was more terrifying than being left alone in the creepy basement.

"We haven't formally met." He approached me and I flinched when he extended his hand. "Donovan Faust." Faust? I had seen that name before in Lush but I couldn't remember in what capacity.

I shook his hand hesitantly, surprised to find it soft, a weird contrast to his seemingly rough personality.

"Rosemary."

"You don't have a last name?" He asked, still holding onto my hand though we were no longer shaking.

I looked down because this was always the weird part of my life. The last name. The foster home had known my real last name but had given me one that I didn't want to claim as my own. I never knew who I belonged to but the person who did know was dead now. Naked and dead.

"N-no, I don't." I didn't want any of these people knowing anything else about me.

"Have you dropped the attitude from last night?" He switched the topic, perhaps sensing my discomfort.

Had I had an attitude? Probably not but I didn't want to piss this man off. As reasonable as he seemed at the moment I was sure that he had a temper far worse than some of my most sexually frustrated clients.

So I answered, "yes" which seemed to please him.

"I apologize on behalf of my right hand. Sometimes he can get carried away with the securing of a zip tie." Nate was his right hand which made a lot of sense considering his semi calculated comments.

"It's okay." Donovan cocked an eyebrow at me.

"Is it?" He challenged.

I gulped not knowing what I did wrong or what to say. It wasn't okay but I was lost for how to respond to him. I wanted to stay on his good side so I wasn't thinking straight.

"Well-no not exac-"

"Lush girls are supposed to be confident. You sure you work there?"

There was no doubt that I was different than many of the Lush girls. Any basic observation on a typical Friday night would show this. But again, he didn't need to know any of that.

"I'm sure." I nodded, noticing that our hands were still in an embrace.

Donovan followed my eyes downward at the sight of my hands shaking from nerves ever so slightly.

"Next time someone brings you to see me, I don't want to see you this nervous ." He was serious. He didn't care that I was anxious, uncomfortable, and scared in this place. He just hated what he perceived to be a lack of confidence.

"There's going to be a next time?" I asked, disillusioned by the hope of returning to my dingy room by tonight.

Donovan squinted and lifted his chin, processing my unintentionally rude question.

"So you haven't dropped the attitude." He still had his hand in mine so he pulled me closer to him, closing the space between us. I took a deep breath.

"No-I did-I was just-"

"Rosemary." He said my name as a demand.

I clamped my mouth shut and felt his grip on my hand loosen.

"Talking too much is what got you here." He said, "So stop."

And with that, Donovan walked around me to the door of the study, leaving me to ponder over his painfully honest words.

Chapter Five: Goodnight Rosemary

Talking was what had gotten me here.

I could've said nothing and swept the whole situation under the same rug that Greene's body was probably rolled up in.

But I talked and now I was stuck.

The next two nights in the basement consisted of me seeing Hannah and several trays of food. When I needed to shower and change, I did so in the basement. I ate in the basement. I slept in the basement. I was slowly dying in the basement.

Hannah stayed with me a majority of the time but never spoke to me about my situation or the activity this obvious crime syndicate ran which was refreshing but also frustrating since I wanted to know who these people were.

Then one evening, after I finished a dinner of steak, mashed potatoes, and string beans, Hannah told me to follow her upstairs. I reluctantly followed since I hadn't been called up since I went to the doctor and formally met Donovan.

"Rosemary, you're a small right?" Hannah asked as she led me up the stairs and through an arched doorway.

"I should be." Although the clothes she'd been brining me were all a size too large. "Where are you taking me?" I asked, feeling tempted to run in the opposite direction.

"Well," Hannah stopped in front of a door. "Donovan is having a meeting with his associates and he requested your presence."

She waited for a reaction from me but when it didn't happen she continued. "He would like you to top their glasses off and keep the platter stocked."

"He wants me to be a waitress?" Being kidnapped wasn't punishment enough to him!

"No, a shot girl or a 'wet girl' like we call it at Lush." I cocked an eyebrow at Hannah. "Wet girl" was a term that only Lush girls used interchangeably with shot girl.

"We?" I asked. Hannah blinked.

"I mean-you. You call it that." She stammered and turned quickly on her four inch heels to open the door we stood in front of.

"Anyway, there are a few pieces of clothing that I picked out for you in the closet in this room. Shower, pick whichever you like and then I'll bring you over to the meeting."

"What if I don't want to be his personal shot girl?"

Hannah looked at me and frowned. "Unfortunately, with Donovan, there are no choices."

"Ever?" I asked dumbly. Hannah put on a tight smile and lowered her tone while stepping closer to me.

"Rosemary, this place and this operation are ruthless and the best way to avoid getting into trouble is to cooperate."

Those words were worthy of a full body shiver and her tone made me not want to ask any further questions. I gulped and nodded slowly.

"Don't stress though. I think Donovan likes you." She smirked. I rolled my eyes at the thought and opened the door to enter the luxuriously decorated vanity room.   • • • •

• •Walking around in scantly clad clothing was the usual at Lush, but this felt different.

Maybe it was the fact that I was being forced to wear these clothes. Or maybe it was because they were La Perla which I'd never owned because I didn't make enough to even look at their lingerie. When Hannah had said she picked out clothes I assumed Salvation Army at best. I wasn't expecting designer choices with the tag still dangling on each piece.

Regardless, I wasn't comfortable in this complex black body suit that I had to pair with heels because apparently that's what Donovan's men liked to see. However, I draped a small white shirt over just to ensure some level of modesty.

Why was this part of the request? I didn't need my ass to hang out in order to pour vodka in a glass.

"How long do I have to be in there for?" I asked when we stopped outside wooden double doors with a bronze engraved plaque that had an "F" written in elaborate script.

"As long as Donovan requests."

"So this can take all night?" Hannah didn't respond. She simply knocked on the door and then after a second she opened both doors.

"Sorry to intrude, but Rosemary's here." She waved me inside the room.

"The bar is by the wall. Shut the door as you leave Hannah." I heard Donovan say.

As I entered I noticed ten or fifteen men around an oval table in the center of the room with Donovan at the head. Though I knew all the men had their eyes locked on me I could feel Donovan's eyes specifically. Following me as I traveled to the bar to service his band of criminals.

I found this room to be less cozy than his study. A large window was on the wall opposite the door but a pair of heavy deep blue blinds were pulled as to not let an obnoxious amount of natural light filter in during the day time. The wall behind Donovan had a built in screen that projected a logo of the same script "F" that was on the door. There were neatly lined numbered shelves around the screen that I assumed held documents since I'd seen something like it in Roth's office.

However, my curiosity and admiration stopped when I noticed a large Doberman Pincher perched right beside the bar.

I yelped and staggered back, falling into the lap of one of the men at the table who had turned his seat around to acknowledge the sound I had made.

"Mmm, baby you're gonna make my pants tight." The man said close to my ear which made me bolt up off of his perverted lap.

"I-the dog was-"

"Stone." Donovan called, alerting the Doberman Pincher that stood and ran past me to find a place right beside the boss.

I breathed a sigh of relief and approached the bar slowly as to not excite the biggest dog I'd ever come in contact with.

"Where were we?"

"Security at The Coral Club." I heard Nate say.

I glanced up to get an idea of what the drink of the evening was and quite simply, most had a caramel colored liquid in their glasses which I presumed to be an aged scotch.

When I was a wet girl at Lush I avoided mixing drinks at all costs. If a customer didn't want tequila, vodka, whiskey, scotch, or wine then I wasn't the girl for them. So my task tonight would be cake.

I filled five glasses and walked over to the table to dole out each to those who had finished their drinks.

"Great piece of ass you got here Donovan." A full figured man said as I leaned over him to take an empty glass.

"I'm sure she appreciates the compliment. Moving for-"

"She didn't say thank you though." I looked over my shoulder with my eyes narrowed. Did this chubby piece of shit just admit that he expected me to thank him? For a vulgar comment? I'd endured many crude comments from clients at Lush but they knew that a tight smile was the appropriate response.

I glanced at Donovan to interject but he just leaned back and returned my gaze.

"Oh, I see, you know you look good so you expect to get compliments and probably an ass pinch."

"No-I-don't know what you're talking about."

"Look, sit on my lap and maybe we can put this whole thing behind us." He winked.

"What?!"

"Sit on my lap."

"No!"

"Moving forward." Donovan said in a loud but steady tone that made all heads shoot up to focus on him. "If I'm interrupted again someone's getting on their knees to apologize." He said sternly. I had a strong feeling that he was actually threatening his own men and not me which felt partially good.

"Now, Anthony I need you to collect from Lush tomorrow night. Tell Roth if both payments aren't in then we're pulling out all security."

Donovan operates Lush? So they were the higher ups of the club.

"Boss, what're we doing with Greene's network?" At the sound of his name I looked up and caught Donovan's eyes.

"We'll talk about Greene tomorrow." He said, locking eyes with me as well. "Tonight is protection and security only." He gave me the slightest smirk and then turned his attention to Nate who loosened his tie before speaking.

I gulped hard at the possible topics that could circulate around my former client.

The meeting was over after two hours of me refilling glasses and flinching every time Stone so much as wagged his tail.

I didn't receive any more harassing remarks which was quite pleasant since my discomfort in this attire only increased by the minute.

When all of the men had filed out a the end of the meeting, it was just Donovan, Stone, and I left where the only sound was the clinking of empty glasses as I collected them from the table and Donovan gathered a stray folder and filed it away.

"Rosemary," Donovan walked around the table and opened the door so that we could both exit. "Is serving my men drinks a difficult task for you." He wasn't asking. He was making a statement that I could answer if I dared to.

"No."

"Are you sure? Because if it is then I can have you serve them in a different way." He stated. "A way that you're probably more accustom to."

Did he talk to every Lush girl like this? Like we were prostitutes? Or was it just me since holding me captive was only the start of his humiliation.

I scoffed at him. "I didn't feel comfortable in this." I said pointing to the bottom part of my body. "And your men were rude." I admitted since I might have been accustom to their behavior but that didn't mean I liked it.

"It's no different from what you do at Lush."

"Lush is my choice." I said without thinking twice about answering him so aggressively. "I-I choose to work there and they take care of me. You don't since I don't have a proper bed or bathroom." I finally said, crossing my arms over my chest which actually gave me a chance to cover my nipple imprint.

I hated that mattress and I hated the odd sized bathroom in the basement that held a bar of unscented soap and a shower head that spouted steaming hot water that could easily put lava to shame. I hated this entire situation and I hated Donovan more for keeping me here.

"Would you like those?" I heard him say.

"Huh?"

"Would you like a proper bed and a bathroom?"

"I would like to go home."

"That wasn't what I asked." He took a step closer to me.

Although my face fell, I knew that I should still consider and give him an answer to his actual question.

"Yes please." I finally said.

Donovan gave me a short nod then motioned for me to follow him down the hall.

It felt odd walking by other people practically naked but I tried not to pay my internal embarrassment to much mind. I didn't know where Donovan was taking me, but I could only hope that it was a notch better than a basement. Maybe it was the attic with a small window for ventilation. Or maybe a walk-in closet with a bunch of old T-shirt's I could fashion into a cot. This place was huge so I wouldn't mind settling for a pantry if it came to that. I clearly wasn't going home any time soon.

Donovan brought me into an elevator and we traveled to level three which seemed to be the floor that was the most homely.

Since being held here all I'd seen were offices, conference rooms, and studies on the first two floors but this was where he probably lived since it was much more personable with carpeted floors, Wall decor, and the scent of fresh linen.

He led me down the hall where he pushed open the last door and motioned for me to enter.

I peaked in and looked up at him for confirmation.

"Are you going inside?" He asked, taking a few steps away from the door. I shook my head and continued to admire from the outside.

There was a full sized bed right under a bay window, a soft beige carpet spread throughout, soft yellow walls, a classic cherrywood night stand, and a copper colored chandelier dangling from the roof.

"Why're you showing me this?"

"I'm showing you what you asked for. There's a bathroom through that door and a closet through that one." He pointed in opposite directions. "I'll have sheets brought up later." He turned to me. "You can stay here for the time being."

I looked up at him. "How long is 'the time being'?" I asked, biting my bottom lip in anticipation of the answer.

Donovan kept his gaze hard on me then I noticed his lips curve upward into a smirk. "Goodnight Rosemary." He turned to walk out but I caught his arm.

"Wait." His green eyes followed my weak grip and I quickly pulled my hand away. "Please."

"Yes?"

"I need clothes to sleep in and can I get my purse back?" I hadn't seen my purse in three days. It had my cell phone which I assumed they knew about since they'd yet to offer my own belongings to me.

"You don't want to sleep in that?" He asked, eyeing me from head to toe.

"Seriously?"

"I like it." He didn't bother to close the door behind him as he closed the space between us. I tried to step back but Donovan took my hand to stop me. He let his fingers travel up the length of my arm and then slowly down to my hips. Then without moving his head, he looked at me.

"I think you're scared of me" His husky voice teased as he caressed my waist delicately with his firm hand.

"I-I'm not." I stuttered the lie in one breath.

Donovan smirked, tightening his grip. I pressed my lips together trying to contain my arousal. He was only touching my waist! Not my breasts, not my nipples, not my ass and yet I was getting turned on.

His menacing jade eyes locked with mine as he spoke, "Right, you're just scared to get fucked by me."

I almost gasped aloud at what he'd said. Why would he even mention that? It was all a mind game for him. He was teasing me because he knew that this was his domain and I had to submit. He didn't care that I was scared and turned on by him.

I bit down on my lip. "Please stop." I summoned the courage to unconvincingly whisper this command despite my body reacting lustfully to his touch.

But Donovan was receptive of my stammered command and he moved his hands away from me with an expression of satisfaction.

"I'll send Hannah to bring you what you need." He said then as my head was down I heard the door shut and I noticed he was gone, leaving me aroused from just the touch of his hand on my skin.

CHAPTER SIX: THE GREAT ESCAPE

That night I had a hard time settling in due to the anxious feeling of being trapped, despite this room being considerably more comfortable than the basement.

I needed to leave my situation, whatever my current situation was. There had to be a way out.

I threw my legs over the bed and stood up. I wasn't in a basement anymore and there was a door right in front of me. I was sure that I remembered the route to get to this bedroom so I could find my way out.

Sure there would be some weary staff walking about but my quick thinking skills were quite impressive. I'd found over fifty excuses to not go to hotels with the men of Lush, so I could find one for right now.

I turned the door knob slowly and took a deep breath. It was unlocked! Donovan was clearly an idiot since-

"Can we help you ma'am?" A baritone voice asked. I gasped up at the presence of two men in dark attire right outside of the door.

"Um-well, no not really. I-" my so called quick thinking skills were on vacation because I couldn't even think clearly. Donovan had ordered guards to ensure that I didn't leave. He was truly a sick and controlling man.

"Please return to bed."

"No, wait! I came out here to-to use the bathroom." I cursed myself for being such an idiot.

"There's a bathroom in your room." One of the guards voluntarily shut the bedroom door. Not even a "goodnight". Well, I guess I didn't deserve one since I'd just made their job harder.

I rolled my eyes at nothing in particular then crossed my arms over my chest. There had to be a way out of this place. It wasn't Alcatraz or some type of full proof dungeon, but clearly the man in charge had been inspired by The Great Escape because there was no way to get out.

As I began to feel discouraged while pacing the room, I glanced up at the window above the bed. Was it at all possible? Unlike the basement, I had access to windows large enough to wiggle through.

I climbed onto the bed and peered out. I was three stories above the ground so there was no possible way to jump. But there was and elaborate vine that connected to a rusted fire escape. The cool autumn breeze might pose as an obstacle for my use of the vine but I was ready to go. I had to take a chance or I would die here.

So I slipped on my shoes and stuck my legs outside the window. It was much scarier hanging freely, but I was determined. I exhaled deeply then reached for the surprisingly strong tangled vine outside the window.

I had to move fast if I wanted to avoid the plant snapping so I swung like Spider woman to get onto the fire escape.

It wasn't the most stable and that was probably because it was the oldest edition to the mansion but it was all I was working with. So I moved slowly to proceed downward.

The second level had a window with the blinds pulled and I knew being seen by just about anybody would be the end of this escape plan. So I pushed my back against the wall and peaked inside the window to see if anyone was facing me.

But as quickly as I did this I gasped at the sight. A man's naked toned figure was pounding a woman from behind in a traditional doggy style position. The man threw his head back and I noticed it was Nate! Then, as if on cue, the woman glanced over her shoulder and I was surprised to see Hannah biting her bottom lip.

"Just keep going Rosemary." I said to myself, hurrying past the window and continuing down the fire escape. It was none of my business who was fucking who in this place just as long as I wasn't forced to do it.

I finally got to the bottom ladder and my body dangled a few feet from the ground. It was entirely too rusted and after contemplating the noise factor I gave up and fell to the grassy ground, feeling the pain of the fall in my leg and my left arm.

I looked up to make sure that no one heard my fall. Satisfied with my mental "all clear", I figured I would fight through the pain I was feeling from the fall and just run away.

So I stood up, dusted myself off, and started toward the darkness. • • • • • •I was beginning to approach flickering nightclub and restaurant lights while continuing to approach the many sounds of nightlife in New York City.

There were some people around which reassured me, but also brought on a hint of anxiety.

My foster home had always been packed so too many people around me was never a good idea. I hated searching for a place to be. It never turned out well and I spent so much time wondering where I would settle just for the night.

"Hey gorgeous." A voice said behind me. I didn't bother to turn around. This happened often and I preferred to not acknowledge men who assumed I was a prostitute.

"How much for the night?" He asked. I sped up my pace but instantly felt a hand grab my arm and spin me around. "I'd like to take you home." He was a tall man with a bald head and smelled as if he'd just bathed in nicotine.

"I'm not a prostitute. Sorry." I pulled my arm away.

"Bullshit. How about a hundred?" One hundred dollars?! Sure I wasn't a prostitute but even I knew that amount was a complete scam. Did he really think that low of me or any woman for that matter? No woman or man should be having sex with random people for a hundred dollars.

"How 'bout you keep your hundred and leave me alone." I snapped, insulted by this smelly man. He narrowed his eyes and grabbed me again.

"You're a difficult one huh?" He pushed me back and I stumbled into a brick wall, dropping my suitcase. "Maybe I should keep my money, take you down this alley and fuck you on a dumpster like the piece of trash you probably are." His face was a mere inch from mine.

The imagery was disgusting and my fear of having to succumb to such a horrid sexual act caused me to push him hard with both of my hands, grab my suitcase, and go running down the street nearly colliding with a taller figure only a couple feet away from the scene of the crime.

"There you are. Roth is waiting for you inside." The body said. I came face-to-face with a headfull of straight red hair and almond shaped brown eyes that illuminated under the glow of the street lamp.

"Huh?" I asked.

The woman looked behind me and placed her hands on her hips.

"Can I help you sir?" I followed her eyes to see the man who had taken me for a prostitute only an arms length away.

He looked between me and the tall woman and then held his arms up in a mock surrender.

"No, I was just leaving to-"

"Great. Now, you know Roth doesn't like to wait so let's go." The woman gave me a reassuring look and took my hand to guide me around to the back of a building with large neon purple words that read Lush in cursive.

"What a pig." She scoffed, pulling open a door of steel.

"I don't know him."

"Clearly." She started guiding me down a hallway with soft white light and walls lined with modern day pin up model images. "The least he could've done was offer you more cash."

"You heard that?"

"I heard and saw everything. Who offers anything less than two? Such an ameatuer." She laughed.

"Oh no, I'm not an escort or anything. I was-"I shrugged, "-I was lost."

"Ah, then I brought you to the right place." The woman winked at me and fixed the leather bustier she wore. She turned her entire body around to face me and stopped. "Charlotte." She smiled, knocking on the door at the end of what seemed like a never ending hallway.

"Rosemary."

"Well, Rosemary, Roth'll help you out since you're..." she scanned me up and down, "...lost. We needed a new shot girl anyway. Daisy got scooped up by some Marine last week so we're desperate." Charlotte sighed, knocking once more.

"I don't even know what this place is." I admitted. Charlotte smirked.

"I like you." She said as a muffled voice sounded from the other side of the door. "And so will the men you meet here."

CHAPTER SEVEN: COOL OFF

The prison of a mansion that I'd been in was in the middle of nowhere. I'd expected to come in contact with another home of similar size eventually, but instead I'd been walking through the woods for the past hour, stepping over fallen trees, and straining my eyes to see ahead.

I was quite use to being on my own so that wasn't the problem. The problem was that I'd never been in such a setting where buildings and street lamps were replaced with pine trees and the soft moonlight glow.

Regardless of my tired trek, I was glad to finally be out of that man's possession. I didn't care how long it took me to find some form of help. The most important thing on my mind was avoiding capture so that I could just go back to Lush, earn some money, and pay my half of the rent for the shitty apartment Charlotte and I shared with other unmotivated degenerates. Lush life was simple enough, as some of the girls would say. I didn't agree but it wasn't my job to have an opinion.

Suddenly I stopped in my tracks and quieted my breathing. There was a sound in the distance that sounded like a faint swoosh. Rubber against the pavement? A road? If there was a road then there were cars with people! People that could save her.

I started jogging toward the sounds and saw a yellow glow pass above which made my heart speed. I had to get up the hill to the road.

I began to work my way up, grabbing at branches and sinking my feet into heaps of dirt. My hands and legs were getting scratched but that was a small price to pay for freedom. I would be saved soon enough! It was a steep hill but it wasn't long and despite being tired I had to make it to the top.

With one final hoist, my body came in contact with a metal traffic barrier. I leaned over it, out of breath and exhausted.

Another car had to pass at some point. Right? I was tired and thirsty which made sense since I hadn't eaten since before serving drinks in the evening. I'd rejected dinner but I regretted the stubborn choice at this very moment since I needed something. Water seemed like such a delicacy right now. As if it were level with veal and caviar.

"Ma'am, ma'am!" A voice said a few feet away.

I glanced up and a thin stream of light was shining down on me.

How long had I been in my water daze? I hadn't noticed another presence.

"Ma'am, are you okay?" The voice asked, nearing closer to me. I squinted and covered the glare of the flashlight with my hands.

"I'm not-I'm not okay. Can you please help me?" I asked, still leaned over the barrier while squinting.

"Yes, but can I help you up first?" I nodded and pushed up, allowing him to take my arm as he turned off the flashlight. I was face to face with an older man dressed in a tan uniform.

"W-wait are you a police officer?" I asked, stopping us both as we approached a vehicle.

"Sheriff. Let me bring you to the car so that you can sit and tell me what I can do to help you." He led me to it and a wave of relief encompassed me.

"Thank you for stopping." I settled into the backseat and leaned my head back. "A man was holding me hostage in his house not too far away. I managed to get out and I've been walking for about an hour-until-until-" I took a deep breath.

"Until I stopped." The Sheriff said reassuringly with a warm smile.

I nodded and he shut the back door.

He slid behind the wheel and started the car. "I have to take you to the station to fill out a report. Then I'll take you home-wherever that is."

I tuned him out slowly as my eyes got heavy. I didn't realize how tired I was until now. My legs and hands burned from the scrapes but I was happy to be safe from Mr. Faust.

• • • • • •

When I woke up I was behind bars.

I threw the thin blanket aside and gripped the cold metal bars shaking them hard.

A corner cell, desks covered with supplies, insignia on the wall. I was in a jailhouse where a slight ray of sun poured in from a small window above the water cooler.

Water! Did I ever get a glass? Probably not since I was parched and my energy was at an all time low.

But why was I behind bars when I was the victim? Had I done something last night in the back of the cop car? Like admit to a crime I didn't commit! Sure Lush wasn't the most dignified establishment but it was totally legal and I'd never gotten in trouble. Or maybe-.

I hit my head on the bar and sighed.

Steven Greene.

They had traced me to Greene's murder and it was all over. If I thought my situation with Donovan had been bad then I was in for a real treat.

"I didn't do it." I pleaded aloud, gripping the bars tighter.

"Didn't do what?" A familiar voice asked.

I gasped and pushed my face closer to the bars to see better as the Sheriff that had rescued me came into view.

"Well-uh," I noticed his confused squint, "whatever you have me in here for. Can you take me home please?" I switched my tone.

"Where's home?"

"Manhattan, the Lower East Side."

He chuckled, setting his mug down on a desk. "You're quite far from Manhattan, darling."

Then where was I? Because clearly I wasn't here because of what happened to Greene.

"Why am I in here?" I finally asked.

The Sheriff handed me a plastic cup of water and shook his head.

"I was told to keep you here for now."

"You were told to keep me here? By who?" I asked, confused.

The Sheriff nodded and sat behind the desk with a grunt. He was the man in charge so who could have told him what to do? Was I not acquainted with the law well enough or was he not a real Sheriff.

"What did you say your name was darling?"

"I didn't say. But it's-"

"Rosemary." A deep voice said right on cue.

I jumped at the sound and my heart began to race uncontrollably as I heard footsteps approach slowly. I did a silent prayer because I didn't want it to be-

"Mr. Faust, is this your girl?" The Sheriff asked, pointing to me and taking a sip from his mug.

I gasped and squeezed the bars tighter until my knuckles turned white.

Donovan and Nate sauntered slowly into my line of sight. Both wore pressed black suits which added to my anxious feeling of unsuccessfully escaping these powerful men.

Donovan stepped closer to the cell with an assertive but arrogant expression. He was thrilled to have caught me and knew I was embarrassed. He was prepared to bask in this moment and I couldn't blame him.

"You thought this was a good idea?"

"I did. But I'm realizing it wasn't a good idea at all."

"Because you got caught."

I looked at him with a twisted expression. I'd only gotten caught because he had the power to keep the police on his pay roll. Otherwise, I would've had a fighting chance at the very least. But I couldn't let him see me sweat.

"Please get me out of here." I tried to ask as calmly as possible.

"You make demands now?" He cocked an eyebrow and turned slightly. "Hey Nate, she makes demands now." Nate laughed, leaning against the desk.

"Be careful, you're not in charge of anything." Nate said.

"I'm in charge of myself. So please get me out of here and I promise I won't run away again." I didn't mean that but I wanted to get out. I'd try every single night to escape if given the opportunity.

"If I get you out of that cell-" Donovan took a step closer to the bars, "Do you promise to-behave." He was being condescending but I didn't care.

"Yes, I promise." I lied.

Donovan stared me down then smirked.

"Like a good little whore?" With that last statement I completely lost my cool and acted out, reaching through the bars to try and grab him. But he backed up with one step and gave me a disappointed look with his eyes now narrowed.

"You know what Sheriff, she needs to cool off in here." He said quite calmly, expecting my astonished expression.

Donovan motioned to have Nate follow his lead to the exit.

"No, Donovan don't leave me here!" I was pleading, "I'm sorry!" I yelled, but by the time I finished my plea, he and Nate were gone and all I heard were their expensive shoes echoing farther and farther away from my desperate cell.

CHAPTER EIGHT: IN TROUBLE

I stayed up for twelve hours in that cell. Officers occasionally came to feed me but all I had was water and an applesauce cup. I didn't want to eat because knowing that Donovan was essentially mocking me was frustrating. He was putting me in my place so that he could control me and make me more submissive than Lush had conditioned me to be.

I knew it was easy for him and it was easy for me to obey most of the time. I'd grown up taking orders and the clients at Lush praised obedient behavior. The best girls were the ones who took the most shit and didn't make a big deal out of it-in front of the clients.

My eyes grew heavy again but I heard footsteps down the hall which conjured up mixed feeling of fear and optimism.

To my surprise, Nate appeared and used a thick key to unlock the gate that enclosed my cell.

"C'mon." He placed the key in his pocket and waved for me to get up. I slowly stood and slid out of the horrible cell.

Nate took long strides and I hurried to catch up. Officers nodded at him as we went through the exit and headed outside to a cool night breeze. They controlled some of the most powerfully corrupt forces and that scared me more than being held against my will because no one could save me if they took orders from the very person holding me hostage.

It was probably eleven o'clock by now and I was easily regretting my hunger strike now that I was out of the cell. If I ended up seeing him tonight, Donovan would surely scold me for not eating.

"Hurry up Rosemary." Nate had the door to a black Audi open, waiting for me to get in. I hurried over, nearly tripping on my own feet. Nate got behind the wheel once I was in and turned to me.

"I'm only going to tell you this once. Don't try a damn thing with me. Don't try and jump out, or scream, or whatever shit you might be thinking. Stay quiet or I'll shove you in the trunk." He didn't wait for my confirmation as he pulled off and started down the road.

Nate drove fast, as if he were racing with an imaginary NASCAR driver. But there was no point in saying anything. Actually, I couldn't say anything or I would be squeezed into the trunk of this luxury car.

A vibration sound buzzed near the dashboard. Nate grabbed his phone and answered. "Good evening Boss...Yes...She is...Are you sure?...yeah...okay ten minutes." He removed his phone from his ear and took a sharp turn.

When we pulled into a vacant lot I noticed Donovan leaned against a black Mercedes Benz. My breath caught in my throat and I sat forward in my seat. I hated Nate but at least I could feel him out which was why I didn't mind staying in this car. But Donovan, was completely unpredictable.

"Get out." I hurried out of the car, wincing a bit at the pain coasting through my body from last night's escapades.

"Farrenger is in the lobby and Lance should be on his way there." Donovan handed Nate a thin folder. "Tell them we're sorry for their-loss."

Nate let out a scoff then asked, "Is he alone?"

"Farrenger should be there with Ashton."

"What if Ashton asks for you?" Nate cocked an eyebrow.

Donovan looked down at me and said, "Tell him I'm busy."

"I'll give you a call when the agreement is done" Nate stepped away to return to his car.

I looked at Donovan wondering what he meant by "busy" but he was already on the passengers side, holding the door open. My only option was to go inside the car despite my fear. So I did, and felt a tear roll down my cheek.

These were criminals and I was their captive. Furthermore, the "Boss" despised me and would do everything in his power to make me miserable. He could just let me go and trust that I would never mention Steven Greene again. But that would be too easy, too simple, and too much of a deal for me. Like I'd always told myself, I never got lucky.

Donovan got behind the drivers wheel and pulled away from the vacant lot. I turned to look out the window and tried to cry silently but that was close to impossible as there was no way to hide my sniffling. Furthermore my stomach was growling like a beast. Donovan was definitely satisfied with my reaction. He knew he'd broke me.

"You're back in the basement." He said firmly.

I was barely surprised. He had wanted me down there all along.

"Did they feed you in the jail?" I looked at Donovan a bit surprised that he'd asked me a question. "Are you going to answer?"

"They-they did."

"But you were too stubborn to eat." He wasn't asking but I responded anyway.

"No, I was-" I sighed. What was the point of even explaining. He didn't care about my wellbeing. "When can I go back home?" I blurted after a few seconds of silence. As quick as it was asked, I wished I could take it back.

"You know the answer to that." He said in a low tone and took a sharp turn with only one hand on the wheel.

I inhaled deeply and focused my attention back outside. It was dark on this road and there were no streetlights which was particularly surprising since I wondered what type of backroad this was and who used it. We seemed to be so far from my prison so not only had I walked far last night, but the Sheriff must've driven me quite the ways.

But Donovan knew that I knew that running away again was a bad idea. My body would be dumped in the Hudson River if I tried it again. No one would look for me. I didn't have family that cared and no one at Lush seemed to care about my current disappearance. Then again, Roth only cared about the girls that made money. If I wasn't at the club then I wasn't making money. If no money was being made then I was useless.

Since Charlotte was essentially the one who had gotten me in this predicament by telling Anthony, maybe I didn't care about Lush either. But it was a safe place for me and it was familiar. I liked familiar because my whole life had been consumed by spontaneity and disappointment.

• • • • • •

"Shot girl!" I sighed heavily at the sound of Mr. Luther's voice near the stage.

I was slowly realizing that being a wet girl meant you were virtually nameless and got little to no privileges compared to the other girls. Maybe it was the fact that we wore the most clothes. And by "the most" I meant instead of laced panties and padded bras we wore shorts and crop tops around the club.

The tips were horrid for a wet girl at Lush and we were forced to stay behind and clean up empty glasses and cigarette butts.

"Two shots of tequila for me and this sex kitten." He snapped, keeping his eyes on Cindy who giggled and twirled her black curls.

I poured two shots with what was left in the tequila bottle then went to the bar to refill.

"How's it going new girl?" Charlotte asked, nursing a rum and coke. I rolled my eyes, setting the empty bottle aside.

"It's hard."

"That's an understatement." She laughed.

"I'm assuming you know."

"The first month is always hard but it'll ease up."

"I mean it's hard being a shot girl."

"Oh that? Well that never eases up." She shrugged and waved her hand.

"What do you mean?"

"Don't you see?" Charlotte put her glass on a coaster. "Who was a wet girl with you during your first week?" I thought back to three weeks ago.

"It was me, Destiny, Monica, Cindy, and Silver."

"Okay, now by this week, which girls became Lush Girls?"

"Cindy and Destiny."

"And have you seen them lately? They're coming to work in Chanel and they don't stay after hours unless they choose to." Charlotte pointed out. I tilted my head. "They became Lush girls Rose and it was for the better."

"But they have to-be with the men."

"So what. We choose how far we go as Lush girls. To be honest, you're one of the longest running wet girls we've had. Most girls drop the shot job within a couple weeks."

"Because the money is elsewhere." I sighed, with a nod. Lush Girls did have it better than us shot girls. Their tips could pay my rent for a month and the work seemed a lot more appreciated.

"Think about it Rose." Charlotte sipped her drink. "Roth is always looking for movers." She winked and walked back to the VIP room where her client was.

I had to think about it at least. I liked keeping my clothes on and not being mandated to accompany any weird men. But I had to consider all the perks of being a Lush girl. It wasn't like I had to have sex with the men. I just had to be around them and keep them company. That wasn't too bad. So I went home and thought about it that night. Thought about being an escort. Thought about being a warm body. Thought about being a whore.

• • • • • •

Donovan reached a tall cast iron gate which slowly opened for the car. Now I was able to see the front of the home that I was held captive in and it was just as large as I'd imagined. It had a contemporary but eerie style which matched the criminal activity that Donovan and his men embraced.

We drove up a long gravel driveway lined with tall trees. The Mansion was such an anomaly though the harsh but classic look matched its owner.

As we neared the front, I noticed about six black vehicles parked and scattered through the driveway in front of the garage. They all clearly loved black cars.

A group of people stood out front, lifting their heads up as the car came in sight. The headlights illuminated the odd scene before us.

Donovan grunted at the sight, slowing the car to a stop as Nate and Hannah's silhouette came into frame and signaled Donovan to come out. He put the car in park and stepped out without shutting the door.

"Nate." Was all he said and probably all he needed to say.

"Lance is with the doctor. Ashton and Farrenger came strapped because they thought you'd be there." Nate shook his head.

"Of course. Let's talk inside-"

"Boss, I hate to interrupt but," He removed a note from his pocket and held it out for Donovan to see. I craned my neck to see past the dashboard but had no luck. Donovan's calm reaction said very little. He bit his lip and nodded.

"They know we're here?"

"We have a big problem Donovan." Nate shoved the paper back in his pocket.

"Hannah, take Rosemary to the guest house."

"Actually, this involves her too."

"It does?" Donovan and I said in astounded unison. The three of them looked in my direction unaware of my eavesdropping.

Nate broke the awkward moment by saying, "Yes, she's in trouble."

CHAPTER NINE: SELFLESS GESTURE

Vote/Comment if you're enjoying the story :)

No time was wasted that night as Donovan and I were escorted into a large black Range Rover and prepared to take a three hour drive to some distant location. That was the only information anyone had shared with me but it was frustrating. I had a right to know why I was a captive that was now going into hiding.

My body was still aching from the previous night and I hadn't eaten in twelve hours at this point. But I kept quiet the entire time since everyone seemed on edge. Especially Donovan who glared out the window with his thumb and index finger touching his stubbled chin.

I looked behind us and saw another Range Rover following closely. Hannah, Nate, and one of the men that had been guarding my room were in that car. Stone was also in the car and it terrified me to think that elephant would probably be with us.

But I could hardly think too hard about the variables of the situation because I was distracted by my hunger. So I settled back in the leather seat and held my stomach.

"Where are we going?" I asked Donovan, but the driver attempted to speak up first.

"We're almost at-"

"No." Donovan finally turned away from the window and looked at me. "No more questions. When we get there Hannah's taking you to the basement and you'll be there until I say otherwise." He cocked an eyebrow. "Got it?"

I pressed my lips together to hold back the choked feeling that I had in my throat, but I nodded regardless because Donovan scared the shit out of me.

"Say 'yes'" He demanded. It was in that moment that I gagged and began to heave from the anxiety.

"St-Stop the-Stop!" I practically yelled, pushing open the door of the car, leaping out, and running to the side of the road to throw up. Nothing but water came out and it was a horrid feeling that made me want to die in that moment.

"Rosemary!" I heard Hannah call as she ran over and placed her hand on my back. "Breathe" she said softly as if I'd forgotten the most essential human function.

I inhaled and exhaled deeply while hunched over trying to rid myself of the anxiety of both the situation and the way Donovan treated me. He hated me, everyone did.

Five minutes passed before I stood up and got a steady pace to my breathing. Donovan and Nate stood undisturbed a few feet away.

"Take a sip." Hannah handed me a bottle of juice which I gulped down.

"Can we get back on the road?" Nate asked, checking his watch.

"Donovan, maybe I should ride with Rosemary?" Hannah asked.

I looked between the two of them. Donovan held my gaze for a split second then nodded and reached to open the door so that Hannah and I could slide into the car. Then he and Nate went into the car behind us and our journey continued.

• • • • • •

"You're in hiding for the time being." Hannah said with a nervous chuckle, walking me slowly through the house that would be my prison for who knows how long. "This is a summer home that Donovan use to bring his favorite girls to so it's meant to be very comfortable."

I didn't want to picture a man that cold utilizing this beautiful place for any romantic reason. It was too tranquil and the layout was exquisite. The outside of the house was a white contemporary style with large windows that seemed to be the result of security measures. The house had nine rooms and a large basement that was the perfect dungeon for my hopeless self. The most alluring feature of the house, however, was that it was located on a private lake and docked two small boats. The boss must've been making millions from his syndicate because I couldn't imagine this type of lifestyle.

"Isn't it beautiful?" Hannah gushed as we looked out from the back porch. I stayed quiet but she knew I agreed. How could I not? My living situations in the past had all consisted of run down apartments or ramshackle houses. This was beyond beautiful.

It was actually therapeutic considering the painfully long car ride and languid state of my body after vomiting. I had nearly passed out when we arrived earlier so Hannah gave me a few crackers to ease my stomach before the tour of the house. Meanwhile Phil, our guard, and Stone, our guard dog, checked the grounds around the house while Donovan and Nate stayed outside to talk logistics.

"Are you staying?" I asked, shoving another cracker in my mouth. Hannah turned to me and gave an apologetic smile.

"No, the rest of us have to run the business and figure out what's going on."

"What's going on?"

"A lot." She shrugged. No one was allowed to tell me anything clearly and it was nerve wracking. "But don't worry, I'll be coming up every few days." She grinned, folding her hands in front of her red pencil skirt.

Hannah seemed to be the only saving grace for me. She told me very little about her personal life and her role in this business but for now all I could do was appreciate her caring about me even in the slightest.

"Okay." I looked back out at the sun rising over the water. We had driven into the morning here and it felt nice to finally see something hopeful.

"Hannah, it's time for you to leave." Donovan announced, appearing on the porch dressed still in his black three piece suit and checkered tie.

I'd only ever seen him in muted settings, but in the natural light he actually had softer features that made him seem a bit more like a human.

Nate was beside him with his hands tucked in the pockets of his gray utility jacket.

"Oh okay, Rosemary I brought clothes to your room upstairs and had the bed made up. Donovan, I cleared the basement like you asked. Was there anything else that needed to be done?" She smiled up at him. Donovan furrowed his brows.

"I asked you to do the opposite Hannah." I was quite confused as well.

"Did you?" She looked astonished. "I'm so sorry. I can call Bill to have the furniture brought down but it'll take a few days." She bit her lip.

Donovan exchanged a look with Nate who hid a laugh behind a cough. I was so confused.

"That won't be necessary." Donovan said simply.

"Perfect. Nate, let's head back. Please stay safe you two." Hannah pulled me in for a hug then followed Nate to the front of the house. Before she turned the corner she gave me a sly wink and I understood exactly what had just happened. She deliberately went against the Boss' orders by stripping the basement of what I needed so that I could have the luxury of staying in an actual bedroom. I felt myself begin to smile at the selfless gesture. I wished, if only for a slight moment, that she would appear again so I could thank her.

"Rosemary!" I heard my name and perked up to look at Donovan who'd been calling me by the back door.

"Sorry, Yes?"

"C'mon, we have some things to discuss." I followed him inside the prison and away from my temporary moment of content.

Chapter Ten: Sitting Duck

The rules of our situation were pretty simple to a person who wasn't here against their will and for reasons unknown. But since that didn't apply to me, the rules of the situation were ridiculously spewed by a ridiculous man who proposed ridiculous things that would make this situation more ridiculous.

"Be up by 8:00 to make breakfast, everything is in the kitchen so there's no need to run out and get anything." Donovan looked up at me without moving his head. "Which reminds me..." He dangled a set of keys and a black quarter sized button before me. "The doors can only open with this so you can only go out if I want you to go out. No more of that running away bullshit."

I wanted to roll my eyes but it would have been a regretful decision so I kept a blank face as I sat across from him at the dining room table.

Everything was so modern and advanced in this house, especially the kitchen that provided and amazing view of the lake so I tried not to get distracted while in conversation.

"A chef will be here for lunch and dinner which you'll help with every day." As if I were a damn housewife. No, I was a Lush girl so I accompanied paying men and engaged in foreplay. I didn't cook for anyone. Not even clients who had a kinky cooking fetish.

"You'll say very little while we're here because there isn't much to talk about."

"Okay." He looked me up and down for a moment and then continued.

"Don't go investigating the house. You're in the bedroom or in the kitchen unless I tell you otherwise." Of course he wanted to make this experience almost exactly like prison. Where was my orange jumpsuit because even he knew that would make this more realistic for us both.

"Okay Donovan." I said, looking away from him. He stood up from the chair and took a step closer to me.

"You're the reason we're here and I've been thinking, maybe killing Greene and you would've been a lot easier." I turned up to look at him through my lashes and gulped hard. "For as long as you're here you'll listen to exactly what I say and you won't ask absurd questions." I cast my eyes down for a moment letting his words sink in but Donovan wasn't done. He tilted my chin up gently with the knuckle of his index finger so that our eyes met again. "If you decide not to comply I'll have you right back in harms way with no one to save you." His finger was still on my chin so I knew he felt my bottom lip quiver a bit from the threat.

I was scared of being alone with him and scared of having to just agree with everything without an opinion.

"Tell me you understand." He asked in a soft but menacing tone that made me shiver.

"I-I think I understand." Satisfied with my response, he gave a short nod then disappeared upstairs without another word.

• • • • • •

The bedroom that Hannah had luckily set me up in was a decent size and had everything that the prison in the other house had except now there was a queen sized bed, pastel blue walls, white bedding, and a silver wall clock. The dresser and closet were filled with clothing and shoes that might or might not fit me.

It wasn't bad but it wasn't home and I just wanted my own bed to lay in. Who knew how long I would be here for the time being. Donovan's room was at the far end of the hallway by the stairs so as long as I stayed out of his way, maybe this wouldn't be too bad. Especially if Stone stayed as far away from me as possible.

That night, after I'd showered and put on the pajama set that was hung in the closet, I laid in the bed and almost had an orgasm at how plush the mattress/sheet combo was.

I'd never slept in a bed this amazing before in my entire life. I almost didn't believe that I was feeling this level of comfort on my backside. Out of sheer surprise, I sprawled my body out like a disc and closed my eyes slowly before falling asleep.

But the merriment was temporary because forty minutes later I heard a thud sound inside of the house which caused me to wake up with a frantic jolt. The thud sounded again and I let out a low shriek. Was someone in the house? Maybe it was that demon dog, Stone. Or even the security guard. The house was large in size so maybe in the dark it was hard to see certain-.Thud!It was followed by the sound of an aggressive knock. Maybe there was an innocent guest at eleven thirty.Thud!I gasped, jumped out of the bed, and swung open the door. The hall was dark and I peered out and saw no one but I heard the knock once more followed by a shaking sound. They were trying to get in! I had to find Phil or Donovan.

I started down the hall peaking behind me and unable to steady my rapid breathing.Thud!"Oh my God!" I was terrified now, I picked up my pace because I knew this was a possible life or death situation. What if I got stabbed tonight? What if the police had a warrant out for me? What if Donovan's crime syndicate was busted? What if this would be the last time I would feel the soft fabric of a queen sized bed in a luxury home. My physical and mental jog was halted by the firm grip on my arm that swung me in a semi circle.

"Ahhh!" I screamed, shaking out of the grip of the burglar, or police officer, or criminal, or whatever the hell-.

"Rosemary, it's me." I recognized the voice and stopped my spasms. "What're you doing?" I shushed him so that the intruder wouldn't hear us. Though my scream definitely didn't help.

"There's someone in the house." I whispered.

"Yeah, you, me, and Phil."

"No, I heard sounds downstairs."

"When?" He chose not to whisper and his deep voice was felt with each word he spoke.

"Just-" thud. I grabbed Donovan's arm. "Now." I could barely see his face but I felt him take my hand off of his arm. Then a moment later I heard the soft click of a gun.

"Stay up here." He said in a lower tone and then I noticed his silhouette move toward the stairs. I wasn't going to stay here alone like a sitting duck. So I hurried behind Donovan who inched down the stairs with what seemed like a metal gun in hand.

He was packing at all times? He slept with a damn gun and now he was going to shoot the intruder?

Donovan looked back at me and gave an eye roll. I apologized with a tight smile but continued to follow him down.

I knew I couldn't handle another gun being fired at a human being but I would take my chances. But where the hell was Phil and Stone? Weren't they the first line of defense in this house?

Donovan was walking close to the wall past the kitchen where the moonlight shone bright against the lake water. I could see way better and again there was a knock but this time it was a lot closer.

"Is that the front door?" I asked. Donovan ignored my question. He stopped by the foyer and stood with his back to the wall. The frosted glass window of the front door showed a dark silhouette that seemed to be shaking the door roughly. The culprit.

"Oh." I was shaking and my heart beat was irregular and rapid. This was really about to happen. Someone else was going to be shot in front of me. I couldn't handle another one, not now!

Donovan pushed me behind him and grabbed the door knob, swinging the door open with the gun held out at chin level. However, what was on the other side was not what had been expected.

"Donovan!" The woman on the other side of the door rose both of her hands. Donovan instantly dropped his weapon to his side and sighed deeply.

"Grace," he shook his head, pulling her inside with one tug and slamming the door closed.

"I'm so sorry, my key didn't work so I was knocking and trying to get the door open." She tucked a piece of brown hair behind her ear.

"The locks were changed." He put the gun on a table with a bowl of mints and ran his fingers through his hair in frustration.

The build up of fear and determination had me on edge as well. She had a key and chose to aggressively find an alternative way into the house.

"I'm sorry Donovan, I should've called but I didn't want to wake you." She said timidly.

"Well," He started toward the kitchen. "I'm awake now Grace." She followed quickly behind him, nearly bumping me as I observed the interaction.

Who was this woman? She was a bit taller than me and had boobs that stood apart from anything else on her body. They were big and fit nicely into her blouse. Lush girls paid a fortune for boobs that perfect.

Donovan went into the kitchen and leaned on the breakfast bar.

"I really am sorry that I woke you both." She flicked on the soft yellow lights and shrugged off her jean jacket. Donovan took it from her and she flashed him a smile as he draped it on the back of a chair.

"I'll have Hannah get you a new key." He said. Grace reached in the fridge and grabbed a mint infused water pitcher, pouring it into three glasses.

"I would appreciate that." She handed me a glass and cocked her head. "I'm sorry that I didn't introduce myself since we're over the initial shock. My name is Grace."

"Rosemary." I said in response, shaking her hand.

"Rosemary, this is the chef you'll be cooking lunch and dinner with every day."

"Chef? That's still a new title for me. I graduated from Le Cordon Bleu last year."

I didn't know exactly why she was telling me all of this but the proper response seemed to be, "Congratulations."

"Thanks!" She smiled. "So you're in this shitty situation with Donovan."

I looked at him for confirmation but he was focused on Grace's movement around the kitchen.

"Yeah, I'm in the room upstairs."

"For now." Donovan said. I glanced at him noticing a very faint smirk form at the corner of his lips. He thought my suffering was funny.

"Well you're still alive so you must be a woman of few words." She partially joked, sipping the water. She was the natural type of attractive. The type that needed a swipe of gloss to go out or the type that wore her features so confidently that it radiated beauty.

"You should follow her lead." Donovan said to Grace.

She put her hand on her heart and pouted.

"I don't speak that much."

"You do." He placed his glass in the sink then stepped beside Grace. Her face flushed a bit at his close approach. "Head upstairs, I'll be there in a few." She bit her lip and nodded. Grace rounded the breakfast bar and touched my back.

"It was great meeting you. I'll see you in the morning." She went upstairs, probably to Donovan's room from the sexual charge of their interaction. He was sleeping with his personal chef? She was beautiful but it seemed like a recipe for death to mess with the leader of a crime syndicate.

"You really don't like to listen." Donovan began.

"I get scared easily." I crossed my arms on the counter.

"Phil roams the grounds with Stone every two hours." He touched his face. "If that ever happens again, knock on my door, tell me the issue, then go right back to the room and stay quiet." He assured with a finalized nod.

"I'll be sure of that next time." I hoped there wasn't a "next time" because this had terrified me enough and I wasn't prepared for another scare.

When I finished my thought process I noticed that I was now alone and Donovan was long gone to ravish his culinary escort.

CHAPTER ELEVEN: CINNAMON

The moaning from the room down the hall was so loud that I was forced to turn up the volume on the radio where some song from The Weeknd was playing.

It was my first day as a Lush girl so now I had access to the second floor dressing room. However, the second floor was also where the Lush class took their special clients for some "one-on-one" time.

"Why is this music so loud?" Charlotte and Skyler came into the dressing room with their ears plugged by their fingers.

"Sorry." I turned the volume down and Ruby's voice echoed.

"Fuck me harder daddy!" We heard her shriek from down the hall.

"Ah, that's why." Skyler laughed and sat on the purple velvet couch. "You look cute." I turned to the full body mirror and frowned at my overly exposed body. The black bralette and teal metallic skirt made me look like a slutty mermaid. I had to look this way though if I wanted more money and freedom.

To be fair, I had the most clothes on in the room. Charlotte had just finished with Anthony and wore only a sheer pink robe with fur slippers. Skyler wasn't part of the Lush class but might as well have been with only a silver bra set under a black kimono.

"Thanks." I took a deep breath. "So I just go downstairs and walk around?"

"Exactly, but stay near the stage, that's where the noveau rich guys sit because they're new to money and want to be see spending it." Charlotte said with a shrug. "Also, don't let anyone order you around like a wet girl." She moved a strand of hair from my face and smiled. "Get some confidence in you and make some money."

Thus, with Charlotte's encouraging words and advice, I descended the stairs in uncomfortable heels and made my way to the front of the club where the elevated stage displayed the Thursday ensemble of amateur strippers grinding their hips to some lyricless beat.

Lush was packed tonight especially since Thursday's were when drink specials were endless. But no one came for the drinks. Clients could nurse a vodka cranberry for five dollars all night and still end up spending two hundred in one hour. They wanted us in their lonely dismal lives and that's all they cared about.

"Hey you!" I heard a voice call. I looked around but couldn't locate the voice until he said, "you with the great ass." His gutteral laugh disgusted me and I noticed his hand wave above his head at a round table full of five other men. Two Lush girls accompanied them.

"Yes?" I said, not use to being spoken to in that manner.

"Get me and my friends another round, would ya." He winked then finished his glass of clear liquid.

"I'm not a wet girl." I rolled my eyes. This was what Charlotte had warned me about and I could tell it would be frustrating.

"Really?" He furrowed his brows. I scoffed and tried to walk away but he caught my skirt by the ends and tugged me back. "Where you going?"

"If you need a shot girl I can get one for-"

"Never mind a shot girl." He turned to his friends. "Someone call over that bitch with the small tits." He patted his lap indicating that he wanted me to sit on it. I almost gagged but I was forced to comply and take a seat.

"I've never seen you before baby." He whispered in my ear, caressing my back.

"I'm new." I partially lied.

"Fresh meat." He chuckled. "I'm bored of the girls here but you, you're different."

"You think so?" I asked knowing exactly what he meant. We all were the same appearance wise: skinny and scantly clad. However, my personality differed greatly.

"I do think so." He reached in the pocket of his black chinos and stood up with me. "Come show me how different you are." He slid three hundred dollars into the waist of my skirt.

"Oh, I'm not a-"

"I know what you are." He laughed and lead me to one of the nooks. "What's your name baby?"

"Uh-it's-" Lush girls all had fake names in order to hide certain parts of themselves from clients. I didn't know what the trend of the names were but using a real name was frowned upon so I thought quick. "It's Cinnamon."

"My favorite spice." He winked and probably lied.

"What's your name?" I asked as we entered the nook together. He sat on the white arm chair and grabbed the bulge in his pants.

"Steven Greene. But I want you to call me Master."

• • • • • •

"Good morning Cinnamon." I looked up wide-eyed from the pan that I was frying turkey bacon in.

"Y-you-how do you know-"

"Cinnamon?" Donovan waved a folder as he sat at the breakfast bar. "You had a pretty good track record at Lush." He closed the folder. "No write ups, no fights, no theft, always on time. Plus, a creative stage name." He said with a slight chuckle.

Was that my Lush employee profile? I was embarrassed that he had access to it as if I were his property.

"I just-made it up on the spot when-" I stopped and scoffed, "when I met Greene."

"Your favorite person."

"He's not my favorite person."

"He wasn't." Donovan corrected. "He's long gone. But from this, it seems that you were Greene's favorite person. He requested you three or four times a week."

I sighed at the memory of Roth giving me personal messages about how Greene wanted me to meet him at his apartment or in his car right before my shift ended.

But why was Donovan reminding me of that terrible man? He'd been nothing short of disgusting every time we interacted. No amount of money could undo the horrible memories I had with Greene.

"Do you want cream and sugar in your coffee?" I asked, setting a plate of food before him. I didn't know how to cook. I never cooked, but I'd picked up some tips at the diner.

"Black is fine." I passed him the mug and looked at the blank folder.

"Did Roth give you that?" Donovan nodded.

"It's called a Lush record." He passed it to me. "We keep them in the office." We? So a conglomeration of people saw this?

I opened the folder and there was a picture of me with my hair tied back. As I figured, very little of my personal information was included since upon arriving at Lush I was unable to provide it. Last name, city of birth, parents name, I didn't know.

Some of my clients were listed on the fourth page which also included how often the single person requested my services.

"So you own Lush but I've never seen you there." I said matter of factly. I'd never seen Nate or Lance either.

"I don't own Lush." He said but didn't correct me as to what his association there was. "And you never had a reason to see me. I have men to run small scale operations." He sipped the coffee and took the folder back.

"Does kidnapping me count as a small scale operation?" I asked a bit peeved at his disposition. It was a bold comment on my part but I wanted to know.

However, Donovan wasn't going to be stumped by my questions. He took the mug and said, "Make sure you clean up." Then he went upstairs.

I groaned, looking at a plate of uneaten food. He could've said "thank you". Actually, what did I expect from this man? He was toxic and his brief moment of conversation with me was only to tease me about my Lush profile.

"Hi Rosemary!" Grace greeted as she entered through the back door in jeans and a scarlette sweatshirt. She had Stone on a leash in front of her. "How did you sleep last night after the scare I gave you?" She giggled. I kept my eyes on Stone.

"Please keep him away from me."

"Stone? Oh he couldn't hurt a fly." She petted his head and grinned detaching the leash and letting him run into the living room. Hopefully he wouldn't feel primitive and return here to eat the leftover food-and me.

"I didn't sleep well." I had to be honest. Her burgular-like actions had terrified me. Being captive also added to the uneasy feeling. "You?"

"I slept great." She gushed flipping her hair off of her shoulder. "Donovan embraced me all night and gave my skin beautifully delicate touches with his lips and with-" she caught herself in a lust filled rant but reeled it back in. "I had a good sleep."

I wanted to shake my head at her schoolgirl admiration of Donovan. He treated everyone else with the utmost respect so I couldn't sympathize at all. Grace seemed like an exaggerator anyway and I was more interested in how she landed this job rather than the perks she got from doing it.

"I'm heading home so unfortunately I can't cook lunch today but I left a lunch recipe in the cabinet above the refrigerator. Start dinner around 5:30 because I'll be back by 6:00. Donovan isn't too picky about food so as long as it's edible he'll be fine." She grabbed her jean jacket and purse then she touched the banister. Grace seemed to contemplate on whether she would go upstairs or not. She shook her head, waved to me, then left the house.

So she was able to maneuver in and out of the house without his key but I couldn't? There had to be another way out. I didn't want to be here even if my life depended on it. Well, I did care about my life but was I really better off here? I highly doubted it.

The rest of the morning consisted of me cleaning around the entire house with very little contact with Donovan. The only time I saw him was when I brought lunch up to his study around noon.

He had been pacing the room while on the phone and the moment I entered he barely gave a glance in my direction. His actions ceased to surprise me because I knew he wasn't impressed with me at all. I wasn't doing anything special while under his roof. I was a bland looking girl that made mediocre meals and was scared of the wolf that roamed the house. I couldn't believe that the next few weeks would be exactly like this. No fun, no money, no personal interaction. Sort of like my foster home when I was four to seventeen. It was suffocating and that's why I always ran away. Because even though my expectations were low and even though I knew any form of shelter was better than no shelter at all, there was always something better and I knew I had to take chances.

Chapter Twelve: Good Girl

I waited until 6:15 for Grace to come help me with dinner, but she had yet to arrive and as time passed so would Donovan's patience. I had no desire to experience what he was capable of on an empty stomach.

So I tried, and failed at what was supposed to be a roasted chicken and potato dish because, an hour into cooking, smoke began to rise from the stove and the smell of burnt meat flowed through the air.

I gasped, grabbing the nearest oven mit and opening the oven door where a gust of gray smoke clouded my view of the poultry.

I coughed, turning my head away and squinting my eyes. How could I have burned dinner? Heating a chicken didn't seem that difficult but within a short moment, Phil appeared, removing the dish from the oven and dropping it into the sink.

The gust of smoke slowly disappeared but Phil turned on the fan to speed up the process.

"Thank you." I muttered with a short sigh.

"You almost burned the house down." Phil stated. No fire alarm had went off so I doubted that the house would have burned down. Dinner did, but the house...? Over exaggerate much?

I placed the oven mit down and hurried to clean the mess I had made. This wasn't my kitchen and though I hated everything about this place, I didn't want to upset anyone.

"What happened?" I jumped at the sudden voice behind me, accidentally dropping the glass plate I held onto the ground where it landed with a loud crash. I yelped, jumping back instinctively.

"Shit!" I cursed, louder than expected and exhaled deeply. I couldn't even look back because I knew that Donovan and Phil were glaring at me. Or maybe they weren't but either way I didn't want to turn.

I felt my throat tighten and could feel tears welling up in my eyes. I wasn't sad, I was frustrated that I couldn't get anything right.

I heard steps coming closer behind me and I shut my eyes tight, ready to be scolded and yelled at.

"Turn around." Donovan demanded. Without hesitation, I did so and came face to face with a calm expressionless demeanor. He looked down at me and continued, "stop crying."

I wasn't crying. I was tearing and trying desperately hard to keep the tears suppressed by biting my lower lip until I tasted metallic.

"What happened Rosemary?" I inhaled a gulp of air. Wasn't it obvious? I screwed up everything.

"I burned the chicken Don-"

"No, what happened to you?" He looked at the sink then back at me. "Are you-off tonight?"

"It's just-" I paused and shook my head. I didn't need to tell him. I'd been "off" the entire time that I was held captive. He knew that so there was no point in repeating this all the damn time. I was stuck. Being a captive was no longer an excuse. "I'm okay." I lied.

Donovan nodded then checked his black leather watch.

"Put some shoes on and come with me."

"Huh?" Donovan turned and didn't bother to address my question. So I hurried out of the messy kitchen to get my sneakers on.

• • • • • •

My impression of the act of "being in hiding" was to keep a low profile and to also keep in a contained area so that your cover wasn't blown.

But apparently those rules didn't apply to Donovan and his crime syndicate since we pulled up to a compact diner in a black luxury car with the driver dressed in a cashmere burgundy pull over and black leather dress shoes. In no way was this incognito but maybe I had a cinematic view of going into hiding.

We walked in and he lead me straight to a booth in the back. It looked nothing like the diner I had once worked at. This place was long and had a dingy ambiance that reminded me of a slasher film setting. Maybe even film noir. The green leather seats of the booth were intact but still felt shrunken and warn. Even the menu on the wall seemed dated in its lettering and dim yellow backlight.

Perhaps I was correct about going incognito because I had a feeling this wasn't Donovan's restaurant of choice and if he could help it, he would've pulled up to The Ritz for an impromptu dinner.

"Order what you want but don't say you're not hungry." Donovan warned, not bothering to open his menu. He was actually doing something for me? A dinner and a choice? I knew this was a treat and I didn't want to cross him. Plus, I was starving!

"Okay." I complied and opened the menu, but paused and looked at him. "I'm sorry for burning the food-and-and dropping the plate." Then I looked back down, but noticed the corner of Donovan's lip slightly curve upward. So he found my clumsy nature amusing.

"'Evenin, what can I get you both?" An older woman asked, clicking her pen on an eight by five inch notepad in preparation.

Donovan looked at me and for the first time I noticed the soft glint behind his eyes that further humanized his character which juxtaposed his primal hostility toward me. It almost eased the nerves my body seemed to produce in his presence. It was clear that he was attractive physically, but that particular glint gave off an air of emotional attraction.

"Rosemary." I was taken out of my trance by Donovan's voice.

"Yes?"

"Order." He pointed to the waitress who stood patiently by.

"Oh uh-I don't-" I stammered. I had to speak more clearly around him. It was ridiculous that I could never get a sentence out. "I don't-know what to order." Now the waitress sighed.

"Do you need more time?" She asked.

I didn't know what I needed. I knew the items on the menu obviously. They were standard diner dishes: hamburger, cheeseburger, chicken fingers, fries, meatloaf, coffee. So why was I all of a sudden frozen in making a choice?

"Can you just bring two cheese steaks, fries, a coke for her and black coffee for me please." Donovan ordered, handing both of our menus to the waitress. She gave a nod before walking away to put in our order.

Donovan leaned back in the booth.

"Sorry-again."

"For?"

"Drawing a blank while ordering." I sighed. "We wouldn't even be here if I hadn't-"

"It was just chicken Rosemary. Stop mentioning it."

"It's a simple dish that I screwed up." Donovan studied me then chuckled.

"I'm assuming you don't cook often."

"I don't cook ever."

"Grace gave you a recipe?" I nodded while toying with the straw on the table.

"She said she'd be back for dinner but..." I trailed off.

"I only told you to cook with Grace so that you had something to do." His eyes looked past me as my coke and his coffee arrived. "Don't worry about it anymore."

It was weird being here with him but as long as we stayed on this general topic I would feel a bit better. How could he be so cruel one moment and then treat me to dinner the next with a new demeanor? I was tempted to ask him the million dollar question of why I had to be in hiding with him but maybe that would be pushing the envelope a bit too much.

However, I didn't mind this Donovan because even though he was still cold he was also likable. Maybe he was just misleading and maybe I was too gullible at the moment, but this was the first time that I felt less worried. Even at Lush I always felt worried that Steven would arrive and request me on a Monday rather than on a Friday just because he could. Or I would worry that my check and tips wouldn't reach a certain amount by the end of two weeks and I would be screwed for a rent payment. More importantly, even though I was twenty one, I worried that the foster system would come back for me and put me with the Bay family again. That miserable family that only kept me around to collect state cash. They didn't care about my pain, my anxiety, my fear. They were just like Steven. Everyone was like Steven.

"Donovan why are you keeping me!" I said aloud out of nowhere which caused the only other pair at the diner to look over at our booth.

Donovan had been looking out the window but he turned to look at me. However, he didn't budge at my outburst. His action made me immediately regret my words.

"Oh no." I gulped. "I have to go to the bathroom." I motioned to get up but Donovan caught my hand. His grip wasn't tight but it was firm and forced me to stay seated.

"Didn't I tell you not to ask me that." It wasn't a question but I nodded as if it were. "You have a hard time listening." He cocked an eyebrow. "Did Greene punish you when you didn't listen?" I pressed my lips together not wanting to revive any memories of punishment. They all were bad.

Donovan removed his hand slowly then stood up from his seat. He hovered over me like an impending nightmare but surprised me when he caressed the back of my neck with his hand then slowly weaved his fingers into my hair. With a light tug, he caused me to focus upward against my will and received an involuntary moan from me. Donovan bit his lip at my reaction.

"We'll fix that listening problem." He tugged harder. "Right?" My lips parted from the exhilarating pressure.

"Y-yes."

"Yes, who?" He asked in a lower tone. I closed my eyes only for a second then corrected myself.

"Yes, Donovan." He narrowed his eyes then released his grip on my hair, giving my chin a gentle touch.

"Good girl."

CHAPTER THIRTEEN: CAT AND MOUSE

Our encounter had left me confused for the night and confusion wasn't a great feeling. He'd done something at that diner to me. He'd come onto me in the most explicit way, by asserting himself further and making me submit to him. It had happened so suddenly but yet so casually, as if it was the suppressed personality of my captor.

But what was worst was that it helped. I'd been in the middle of a minor anxiety attack and he'd been able to stop it. Almost instantly. Usually when I got into my anxiety fits I hid out in the Lush bathroom or completely removed myself from the situation entirely. But this time it just-stopped. As if I'd taken a dosage of medication.

However, the worse of it all was that the entire brief situation had aroused me and I couldn't even lie to myself about it. I hadn't been genuinely aroused since I began work at Lush. It was something about the general atmosphere. The idea that I walked around scantly clad for a demographic of men that ranged between twenty five and near death.

The men were unattractive and something in the way they used se-ductive language made each word gag worthy, "suck me baby" could easily be translated to, "put your mouth on my viagra induced cock." Which only made my job worse. I wasn't even aroused by one-on-one sessions which were supposed to be a bit better. But all those seemed to be was me putting on a play and exaggerating a few moans and groans so they could relieve themselves and pay me a handsome tip. Sort of like the curtsy at the end of a theater production.

Donovan had given me my first mental orgasm and physical arousal in a long time. For so long I thought it impossible but now, well now I was still confused which was evident by the short responses I gave and the silence of the car ride.

"Boss." Phil said, leaning on the window of the driver's side as Donovan pulled up to the lake house after our diner run.

Donovan turned down the radio.

"Something happened. Hannah, Nate, and Lance are on their way up."

"Something?" Donovan shook his head. "Show me."

"Should Rosemary come?" Phil asked.

"Yes." Donovan handed Phil the key and opened the back door. "Rosemary, get in the back." I moved to the backseat of the car, keeping my distance from him for fear that he might make me submit again. He was clearly capable of anything.

Phil drove extremely fast since our destination was relatively far. I expected the aforementioned "something" to be a warehouse full of drugs or even an abandoned house with dead bodies. Instead, we pulled up alongside a silver Porsche stained with several bullet holes.

Donovan was quick to get out of the car with Phil to inspect the exterior and interior. Apparently they knew who this car belonged to and it must've been a big deal. Again, I was out of the loop. That is until Phil reached into the car and pulled out a denim jacket. I hadn't met many people while here in hiding but that jacket was familiar and there was no doubt in my mind that it belonged to someone I'd recently met. Now I knew why dinner's mastermind hadn't arrived.

• • • • • •

Donovan, Nate, Lance, Phil, and a few others were in the dining room having an in depth discussion. Hannah filtered in and out, bringing printed information to Donovan when necessary.

The only reason why she hadn't come to see me was because everyone assumed I was asleep. I felt like a child attempting to watch television after bedtime, just sitting on the stairs and trying to listen closely.

"They shot at her car but didn't kill her?"

"They didn't want to. The gun shots were just to stop her."

"But how did they know her affiliation with us?" Someone asked. I couldn't identify any of the new voices.

"No idea, but the car was only an hour away from here which means they might know we're around."

"Shut up Nate."

"It's true!" I heard Nate say defensively. "We have a small amount of time to figure something out or they'll find the girl." The girl? He knew my name.

"She's causing more trouble than she's worth." I recognized Lance's voice. "It's the reason they're hiding out in the first place." I sighed at his statement. How could I be the reason?

"No, they're hiding out because Donovan volunteered to protect her." Someone mentioned which made my ears perk up.

"True, had you let Nate do it like we originally planned then Ashton would've been cold under the Verrazano." Lance sounded like he was only partially joking.

"So, should we move you to the house upstate?"

"No." I finally heard Donovan speak. "I'm not playing a game of cat and mouse." His voice commanded the room. "I agreed to not go after Ashton because of Rosemary, but my patience is wearing thin. I want one of Ashton's men by the end of this week. I don't care how you find them, just do it or I'll have to step in." There was a silence that engulfed the room. "And while you're at it, find Grace too."

I couldn't believe it! Grace was only his chef and now her life was at risk, if she was still alive. Anyone could be in trouble if they were affiliated with this syndicate. I felt like I was a walking target. There was no way out of this place alive. I was going to die here if I didn't at least try to leave captivity again.

"Get up." I heard Donovan's voice say before me. I hadn't even heard him walk up the stairs alone.

"I couldn't sleep with all the-"

"C'mon." He interrupted as he passed me.

"With you to-" I stopped when he opened the door to his room and held it to wait for me. He was serious about wanting me in there. He did own Lush so he was use to getting his way. I followed his trail and went into the room with a tentative step forward.

• • • • •

"Grace is missing." Donovan poured some dark liquid into two glasses, "That was her car and jacket." He crossed the room to hand me a glass. He knew that I knew but I still made sure to be responsive by nodding and staying in my a lot right by the door of the room.

This gave me a great view of what he was working with in terms of luxury. A space three times the size of the room I'd been put in with sophisticated features and a gray and blue color scheme. I was sure that the wood mini bar with glassware cost more than everything I owned in my locker at Lush.

"How do you know she's not dead?"

"She's the daughter of a senator. She's more valuable alive." He took a sip of the drink. "I'm telling you this because they wanted you." I caught my breath in my throat, feeling my heart almost beat out of my body. Would he have traded me for Grace if he could?

"Really?"

"Someone wants to hurt you Rosemary. If you keep making careless decisions, I won't care if they do." He stepped closer to me and my heart sped up from the space between us closing in distance.

"So why are you protecting me?" I said softly, thinking about what I'd heard him say earlier.

"Because you're useful." He said, stepping so close to me that there was barely enough space for me to take a deep breath.

I could feel my sex begin to moisten from his contact. "You're really close to me." I wanted to say more and he knew it but I just couldn't get the words out with him this close. Looks and body language were key at Lush, so words were never an important factor for me in front of men.

I watched Donovan's face study me closely as if trying to figure out how I felt about him only an inch away. Then the corner of his lips curled up slightly and he took the glass from my hands, setting both down with a hard knock on the dresser.

"So what?" He said quite simply. "If I'm close, tell me to move away." He propositioned, continuing to move forward whil I took short steps back not out of fear but in an effort to protect my own feelings. Physical and mental.

"Can you-" I tried to speak but butterflies formed in the pit of my stomach and my head was light.

"Tell me." He said, loosening his tie from around his neck.

"I-I-"

"You're so scared to speak up for yourself." Donovan shook his head, reading right through me. Before I could fall back onto the bed, he caught my arm and tugged his tie from around his neck, looping it around my wrist and fastening it to the headboard. Now I was restrained.

"What're you doing?" I looked up at him, pulling my arm.

"You know what I'm doing." He spoke close to my face. "This isn't Lush, if you want something you better say it." He kissed my neck and my body shivered. I felt him smile near my delicate skin.

Why was I so turned on? This must have been a lusty version of Stockholm Syndrome because I couldn't contain my sexual responses to him. And he noticed since he looked downward, and with one hand rouched my thigh to part my legs where the evidence was. I was so embarrassed. With my only free hand, I covered my face, disappointed in my body's reaction. He'd been mean for the past few days and yet I had a wet spot seeping through my shorts.

His hand moved between my legs and rubbed the outside of my shorts gently while he continued to kiss my neck and tease me with his commanding tone that challenged me to assert myself.

"Is this how you are with your clients? They tell you what to do and you drip all over yourself." I bit my lip and shook my head. It felt so good.

"No, I don't let them-" I gasped as he rubbed a bit faster and I felt myself nearing completion. "I can't-I can't hold it."

"So cum." He purred in that sultry velvet tone that caused me to convulse and writh as I rode the orgasmic wave that was essentially foreign to my body. I couldn't believe that he'd done that without even touching my actual pussy, or any part of my body for that matter. The thought of the entire situation sent me above and beyond and now I was breathing heavily with one arm tied to the headboard.

Just as Donovan stood up to gaze down at my embarrassed form, a knock sounded at his door. My eyes bulged in shock but Donovan didn't seem concerned. He untied my arm with a single tug of the tie and then went over to the door to open it.

"Donovan, I'm so sorry to interrupt you this late." I heard Hannah's voice on the other side.

"You're not interrupting." He moved aside and Hannah entered. When she saw me she smiled.

"Hi Rosemary, I didn't know you were awake." I nodded, keeping my legs closed tight together. Apparently Donovan thought that had been nothing but my body said otherwise.

"What is it Hannah?"

"Oh yes, Anthony is scoping out the nearby town but we can't get through to him. Nate's not sure why." Donovan cocked an eyebrow but slowly nodded as if he were deep in thought.

"Hannah take Ro-"

"I can take myself." I interrupted, standing up.

Hannah looked stunned at my bold interruption. Donovan put his hands in his pockets and followed my every step with his eyes.

I was upset at how temporarily gulliable I'd been just now. How could I let him tease my emotions in this way knowing full well that he didn't care about me. That was why he wanted me in the basement, that was why he told Hannah she hadn't interrupted anything, that was why I never knew what was happening.

Donovan Faust didn't give a shit about me and allowing him to come this close to me was a clear example of me not learning my lesson from the past.

Chapter Fourteen: Liquid Fantasy

I felt trapped with Steven Greene. He had a hold on my life and I couldn't break free. The only way I could make it through an intense session with Greene was to bite my lip and think about what my life could be. I would never get to a better place but I had to dream.

I felt a sharp sting on my leg and fought back tears.

"Say you're a whore." Steven demanded, a black strap in hand and an arrogant smile splayed on his face.

"I'm-" I took a deep breath and felt the sting again. This time I screamed in response and shook my head from the pain. "I'm a-I'm a whore."

"Yes you are Cinnamon." He laughed, unbuttoning his pants. "Yes you are." • • • • • •I didn't hesitate to speed past Donovan's room, jog down the stairs, and sprint for the back door. I pulled at it and searched for a lock but there wasn't one.

Surrendering easily because of the circumstances, I hurried to the front door but received the same failure. Only the key he had accessed the locks on the doors but I didn't want to be here. I refused to be a target like Grace. Also, Lance had said I was causing more trouble than I was worth so I was clearly worth nothing.

I looked out the window at the lake where a row boat bobbed in the water alongside the dock. If I could get to it fast enough then I would have some mode of transportation to escape.

So without a second thought, I went into the kitchen, grabbed the heavy iron pan that I'd used earlier today, and hurled it at the window causing the glass to crack. I picked it up and glanced behind me to see if I had woken anyone up. The house was full tonight and if anyone caught me then I would be a goner.

After two more dedicated throws of the pan I watched the glass shatter into a thousand pieces. Though just as quickly as it broke, an alarm sounded throughout the house.

I gasped, knowing I had to act fast. I crawled out the window, trying my hardest to not get cut and once I was through I noticed Phil trotting down the steps with Stone by his side.

I started in a full sprint toward the lake, not turning back for even a moment despite hearing my name shouted in the short distance. If I focused forward I could get to the boat and it would be a fight or flight situation. I was okay with that. I just wanted to leave.

But as I felt cold liquid around my ankles and looked ahead I realized that from a distance this had all seemed too easy. But the boat was farther from the dock than expected and my body was instantly iced over as I delved deeper and deeper into the lake water.

I was breathing heavily now and my chest felt as if it were closing. I couldn't do this but I had to. I didn't want to give up now with people chasing me while I was far ahead. But I was chest deep in water and the boat was just a few feet away.

"No." I gasped to myself and reached out to grab the side of the wooden dock. My body was freezing and I felt exhausted. Just one second to get myself together.

I rested my arms on the cold wet wood and after only one breath I noticed two black boots before me. I glanced slowly up at Phil and without a second thought. I screamed and fell back into the water. It engulfed me and I felt as if time had stopped and I was safe. I could see a large silhouette but it couldn't get me. Not if I was frozen in time and emercced in this liquid fantasy that provided a momentary escape.

But the moment ended almost as quickly as it began because the large silhouette lowered and I felt my shirt stretch and pull forward until my entire body was out of the water and brought onto the dock. I keeled over, coughing heavily. I couldn't speak, couldn't protest his actions, I couldn't even jump back in and row away. I shivered uncontrollably and I almost felt as if I could see myself from an alternate perspective looking pitiful under the darkness of the moon.

Phil lifted me bridal style and began to walk toward the house. I didn't fight him. There was no need to when I knew I would lose.

"Phil hurry! She needs to get warm." I could hear Hannah call from a distance. I could even hear panting beside me and assumed that my frenzy had even called for Stone to take action. But had

Donovan come out? Probably not since he didn't care and wanted me to disappear. I tried to give him what he wanted. But somehow I kept getting pulled back.

CHAPTER FIFTEEN: SIX MONTHS

Phil brought me upstairs and set me down on my feet while I continued to shiver. Hannah rushed behind us in confusion.

"Why did you bring her in here Phil?" I was in Donovan's room.

"I was told to bring-"

"Don't start with me. Bring her to her room, she's freezing!"

"Hannah, I can't do-"

"She's freezing!"

"Hannah." A new voice entered the room and both Hannah and Phil clamped their mouths shut. I wrapped my arms around my body, feeling a wave of cold brush past as Donovan entered.

"Can you both leave." It wasn't a question, but his tone was polite. Hannah gave me a final glance before walking out with Phil. She said something to Donovan which caused him to nod.

When they were both gone Donovan shut the door. I would do anything for a blanket or even a towel right now. My entire body was quivering and I could barely feel my lower half.

"You tried again." He cocked an eyebrow. I shook my head and attempted to respond but Donovan was already on the next statement. "Do you even care about your life?"

His words stung in that moment and despite my shivers, I could feel warm tears begin to swell up in my eyes. I gulped hard.

"You-you don't care!" I summoned the courage to say. It hurt more to hear my self saying those words rather than thinking them. It was another person in my life that didn't care but it still hurt. If he didn't care, why did he assume I would. He'd kept me for so long and expected me to stay idly by.

Donovan's stare burned through my core. I didn't know what he was thinking but I knew he was upset.

"Why do you keep running away?" His tone didn't change but something in his question caused the tears to immediately escape from my eyes. I couldn't control my emotions or the feeling of my body giving up. Even the cold couldn't distract me.

Donovan sighed in frustration then grabbed my arm tightly and pulled me to him.

"Why do you always run Rosemary?" His voice was firm and I knew he wasn't only concerned about me running. He didn't understand why I was crying and he didn't understand why I couldn't listen. I knew this because it was what I wondered every single day.

So I broke down and collapsed to my knees, covering my face with my hands. I hadn't wanted anyone here to see me in this pitiful state but Donovan triggered the worse part of my life. The part that had happened not too long ago. • • • • • •I laid my head down on my arms before the vanity mirror and sighed heavily. I'd wasted two hours of service each night for the past two weeks just sitting here and pondering.

Sometimes I was interrupted by some of the girls changing into leather and lace clad attire while listening to an erotic soundtrack that apparently got them in the mood. Other times I was interrupted by a Lush class girl occupying one of the rooms next door and playing on fetishes and kinks that involved loud and exaggerated vocal performances.

The loudest was Charlotte and Anthony which was probably the result of actual affectionate sex that involved the occasional vibrator.

But anything was better than confronting the Devil's spawn. The notorious gremlin that seemed to make my job more difficult. I was still in pain from my session with Greene and the whip and belt so there was no way that I wanted to be near someone who could hurt me that much.

Roth didn't care and Charlotte didn't understand because she was essentially bound to a man that adored and confided in her. We couldn't all be that lucky. She probably knew more about Lush through him than all of us put together.

I grabbed another oatmeal cookie from the basket and took a hearty bite, turning away from the vanity. I didn't need my own reflection judging me. I did it enough.

Ruby came into the dressing room with a grin that wasn't meant for me. She wrapped her silk robe tight around her body when she noticed I was inside.

"Hey Rose." Her cheeks were flushed a bit. I smiled, finishing my cookie.

"Georgio?" I asked. Ruby smiled and nodded. Georgio was a young Italian client, quite handsome and had come for the first time last week. He had a thing for large breasts so Ruby had the luck of servicing him. From the look on her face, he'd ravished her from only a simple fourplay session.

"Yeah we were in the nooks for a while but he had to leave after an hour to do some-business thing." She shrugged then went to approach the bathroom, but stopped right at the door.

"Oh, Greene is downstairs. He's waiting for you." Then she went inside. I rolled my eyes. No one knew I was avoiding him per se but I didn't hide it.

"Rosemary." Silver barged in, her hair coming loose from a once tight bun.

"Yes?" I shoved another cookie in my mouth.

"I've been looking for you." She kicked her heels off. "Greene's here for you." Shit, was he just telling all the girls to inform me.

"Tell him he has to make an appointment." Not that it would make a difference since I'd found a way to avoid him for the past two weeks. I turned back to face the vanity mirror.

"He said he just wants to talk." She shrugged, grabbing a cookie over my shoulder. "Something important."

I considered for a moment if I was willing to see him at all. I didn't like him as a client so why would he "just want to talk" as if we could be two regular individuals. No way, I was Cinnamon and he was Mr. Greene or Master.

I slipped on a pair of heels and felt my eyes roll into my head as I headed downstairs and approached the bar. I noticed him seated with his first three buttons undone and a wet spot on his collared shirt. He had a shot glass between two fingers. When he noticed me, his eyes grew dark and a smirk appeared on his face. I was so use to this expression but today it was more menacing.

"How are you?" I asked dryly. I didn't care how he was. He sold luxury property by day and bought ass and tits by night. I was sure he was the same as usual: rich and horny.

"Great, have a seat baby. Talk to me." He threw back the shot then patted the seat across from him.

"Uh, I can't talk for long." I sat down, not even attempting to continue my excuse. Greene didn't seem to notice as he ordered two more shots.

"To be honest, this talk won't take long-Rosemary."

"Oh great because-wait-" I narrowed my eyes. "How do you know my name?" Steven smirked, sliding a shot glass over to me.

"Well, looks like I got your attention after you avoided me for two weeks." He sighed. "I'm disappointed in you for that." I held my breath. He knew. Not that it was hard to figure out but that wasn't my concern. He knew my name.

"I had other clients."

"No you didn't, but it's fine." He shrugged. "I understand how difficult I must be."

"Is this what you wanted to talk about?" I was confused as to why I was here.

"It is actually." He reached under his stool and grabbed his brief-case. "I'm not upset at you-running from me. Mainly because I real-ized you run from-everything." He pulled a familiar folder from the briefcase and laid it flat on the bar table. I looked down at it and back.

"I-don't know what you mean."

"But you do. And so does the Floyd family and the Bay family." In that moment my pupils dialated and I felt my throat choke up on nothing at all. How the hell did he know who they were?

"What's going one? How do you know those names?" Greene shrugged and cleared his throat.

"Same way I know yours. Actually, I know a lot about you Rose-mary. I just recently did some business with Mr. Bay, you ran away from them before your eighteenth birthday didn't you?" He bit his lip and chuckled. I didn't respond because I was ready to burst from my blood boiling.

"Is that what the folder says?"

"And then some."

"Give me it." I demanded. I recognized that folder because Mr. Bay had once taunted me with it.

"Oh, I will." He nodded quickly. "I have no plans of keeping your personal foster home files baby." My chest tightened from what could possibly be kept in that folder. Everything I wanted to know about my life, about the foster system, about my real family, he had it all.

"What do you want?" I asked with my fists balled.

"Good girl, I didn't even need to tell you to ask me that." He smiled. "Roth is drafting something now. I told him to make you and I an exclusive six month contract. Six months of me having priority over your services."

"Roth would never agree to that!" I gaped.

"I thought not too, but money talks Rosemary. Money always talks." He was right. Roth did anything for the right price and knowing that I wasn't the most in demand Lush girl probably was more of a deal for him.

"Six months?" I asked, my voice quivering at the thought.

"At my beck and call. Then you'll get this." He flicked the folder with two fingers.

I was in awe. Greene had my whole life in his hands and I was powerless against him. There was no way out of the suffocating hold that Lush was responsible for. Steven Greene was the reason that my life became complicated. He was going to make me work for my own identity.

CHAPTER SIXTEEN: NO MODESTY

I was gazing out of the window the next morning, trying to distract myself from the pain that soured through my entire body, when a knock sounded on the door.

"Rosemary?" Hannah poked her head in before she walked into the room dressed in a gentle pink wrap dress. "Good morning. How're you feeling?"

"I'm sorry for causing you trouble."

"No need to apologize. I wouldn't like being-" she stopped, catching herself possibly for fear of making her boss look bad. But nothing could make him look any worse than he already did in my mind. "Um-I know what it feels like to be trapped." She moved a strand of blonde hair that had escaped her bohemian bun.

I said nothing as she began to explain further.

"Lush was my home for two years, or at least I thought it had been my home. Roth and the clients made all the decisions for me." She crossed her arms in front of her timidly and sighed. "Sometimes I wasn't allowed to eat because my wealthiest client had some obscene fetish with gagging." She shook her head.

"You don't have to tell me this." I said quietly, sympathizing with her tremendously.

"I know." Hannah nervously laughed. She was generally so confident and self assured but she was making herself vulnerable. "When I felt trapped I remember some Lush girl telling me her story and it didn't make me feel better about my situation, but it made me feel-safe." She paused. "Nate found me in one of the rooms one night near death from malnourishment. It was an accident but-he saved me." She smiled to herself at the memory. I didn't know what to say. She was someone that I could relate to and I'd never had that before. No one really cared to talk to me about their experiences or tried to make me feel better about my own. Not even Charlotte.

"Hannah, I'm sorry that-"

"We should go." Hannah wiped her eyes with a quick swipe and went to the door. "Donovan's waiting." I followed her out reluctantly and happy that the subject was changed even if it meant facing Donovan again. I wasn't good at consouling others or myself.

She led me out of the house to a partly cloudy morning sky.

Donovan was beside the black Benz with Nate and Lance deep in conversation.

"Donovan, do you need anything else for today?" Hannah asked him, handing over a pad-folio. He looked at me and then looked at her.

"Why're your eyes red?" Lance asked Hannah, leaning forward to get a closer look. Donovan pushed him back in one motion, shooting Lance a warning glare before responding to Hannah.

"No, we should be fine. You can head back to New York."

"New York? No way, the police connected Greene's murder to an organized crime syndicate. Read about it this morning." Lance chuckled.

"Yeah, the Chief said we should lay low for a couple days." The Chief of police? Of course, they had another Police Department paid off.

"I'm laying low in Florida if you're giving us the next few days off Boss." Lance insisted with a shrug.

"I'm not doing that." Donovan rolled his eyes. "Go back to the city and make Ashton's life hell." He said, "when he's quivering under a knife then we'll talk about 'time off'." Donovan smirked, patting Lance on the back.

"Sounds like a plan." Lance walked to the Cadillac at the bottom of the driveway. Hannah gave me a tight smile then followed behind him. Donovan opened the door of the Benz and motioned for me to enter the back seat then slid in after me.

"Nate," Donovan said before he could walk off.

"Yeah Boss?"

"Make sure she's alright." He said and without saying her name we both knew he meant Hannah. Nate nodded his head once then made his way to the Cadillac as well.

Now it was just us again. I didn't know where we were going this morning but I was sure that I had run out of chances with this man. He was probably going to take me to some distant forest to shoot me dead. It was understandable. I was more trouble than not and running into the lake had set off alarms that could have given away the entire hiding initiative. My death was well overdue.

"How do you feel?" Donovan asked.

It caught me off guard and it took me a moment to respond because I figured he'd been talking to Phil. However, he looked at me, awaiting a reply.

"Uh-I feel okay." I said in almost a whisper.

"I'm taking you to a doctor."

"Why?"

"Apparently you have bruises. And-" he touched my hand and turned it. I winced at the pain and for the first time I noticed bandages wrapped around my hand where the glass from the window must've cut me.

"I didn't notice." I looked at his hand on mine and took a deep breath. He followed my gaze then removed his touch.

"You bruise easily don't you?"

"I seem to always find myself in situations where I'm susceptible to them." I sighed, thinking of Greene.

"I should've killed him sooner." Donovan said as if reading my mind. I was going to respond but I noticed him remove his phone from his pocket to answer a call.

• • • • • •

The doctor didn't do much since there wasn't much he could do. He simply asked where I'd gotten my bruises and cuts from to which I lied and stated that I fell down a flight of stairs and broke a glass vase on my way down. It was an absurd lie, and I was sure that I didn't even need to lie given the fact that Donovan wasn't concerned with me saying anything. But the doctor had other patients to tend to so I doubted that he was too concerned with my situation.

Luckily, stitches weren't necessary. Ointment was applied to my cuts after they were cleaned with alcohol and then my hands were bandaged.

"Have an Advil if you start feeling pain." He advised, handing me an individual packet. "Other than that, you're free to leave after you're dressed. I'll let Donovan know." This was another of Donovan's hired professional criminals at an office thirty minutes from the lake house.

When the doctor stepped out, I moved off of the bench and shrugged out of the hospital gown, pulling my jeans on first.

There was a knock on the door and I turned slightly before saying, "Come in." The door opened slightly and I peered over my shoulder to see Donovan. "Sorry, am I taking too long?" I reached for my bra.

"No, the doctor said you called for me." He turned away.

"I didn't." I looked in his direction and almost laughed at his effort to protect my modesty. There was no modesty at Lush. We got naked as a unit and there were a number of times when men walked in on our topless forms.

"Why're you laughing?" He glanced over his shoulder. I caught myself in mid chuckle then flushed red.

"Oh sorry." I turned away again, embarrassed by letting my guard down.

"No, tell me." He said in almost a whisper. I felt him nearing my body and a shiver ran down my spine. His steps were calculated and before I was able to hoist my bra strap over my shoulder, I felt his hand touch my back. My breath quickened and my heart raced.

"Calm down Rosemary." He said, his tall stature hovered over me. His words were said in a tender tone and his hand traveled upward to my shoulder and he pulled at the bra strap, spinning me to face him. I gasped as I stared up at his face. Green eyes studied my features as I continued to breathe unsteadily.

Then he did something that truly caught me off guard, he lifted me and put me on the bench, reaching behind to unclasp bra.

"I want-"

He quieted me with a gentle "shhh" which I found useful since I needed to be told what to do. My body was heating up and I could feel a wet spot form between my legs as Donovan wrapped his hands around my neck and brought me to his lips.

It was the type of good that was so wrong but felt right. My body gradually relaxed at the warm touch of his lips on mine and I almost fell back from the sheer ecstasy coursing through my body.

Just as my body furthered into an erotic state, Donovan moved his lips down my neck and stopped right at my nipple. He looked up at me before flicking his tongue.

"Oh my God!" I moaned. He did it again and it sent me upward as he sucked gently on my nipple. It was exhilarating and I let my finger weave through his blonde hair to show my appreciation further.

"Rosemary." He said.

"Mmmmm" I moaned in reply.

"Rosemary!" He repeated louder and in that moment I leapt into the air and opened my eyes.

I was in the doctors office with only my jeans on. I turned around but Donovan wasn't there. What the hell had I been daydreaming about?

"Rosemary!" I heard him outside of the door, more frustration in his voice as he knocked.

It had been a dream. A lusty, suppressed dream that pitifully displayed a feeling of want. How could I think of him like that? He wasn't here to please me. He'd done it once as a power play but what was I thinking.

I threw on my shirt then swung the door open. My forehead was glistening with sweat and my cheeks were rosy from embarrassment. Donovan stood outside the door with a cocked eyebrow.

"Why did that take so long?" Our eyes met and I swallowed a hard gulp.

"I uh-got-distracted."

CHAPTER SEVENTEEN: IN PLAIN SIGHT

I hated myself for thinking of Donovan sexually in such an inappropriate setting. He didn't like me and he made that very clear everyday. There was no reason for me to think of him in a sexual sense. Sure he was handsome, and powerful, and his presence was prominent, but he was cold.

Looking at him made me realize what many of the Lush clients lacked. They wanted that type of power and they probably wanted the aesthetic attractive features as well. When a man like Donovan entered a place like Lush all the girls flocked with hope that they'd get chosen. Moreover, if Donovan himself entered a place like Lush it would be a field day full of distraction. The push up bras would be adjusted, lipstick reapplied, and flirtation set to 98 percent.

But he was clearly smart about his business at Lush. He probably never entered through the main doors and never stepped foot past the third floor offices. It was the best bet to avoid the female vultures.

"It looks like it's gonna rain." Phil peeked past the dashboard. "You still want to grab lunch at Russo's?" He asked, quickly glancing back.

Donovan leaned forward and nodded.

I was glad that he called the shots in that moment because I hadn't eaten since last night and it was already noon.

Phil pulled into the lot of a restaurant as it began to drizzle.

"Get yourself something but be back in fifteen minutes." Donovan sounded peeved as he stepped out and waited for me to follow. He took my hand and rushed me inside so that we wouldn't get wet.

"Is he not allowed to eat with us?" I asked. Donovan grabbed two menus from the front and then lead us to a booth in the corner.

"He needs to be attentive." We sat down and he slid a menu to me.

"Am I allowed to order something too?" Donovan gave me a twisted look.

"Is that a serious question?"

"Well-yeah I-"

"Rosemary, just order what you want please." He shook his head. His response put the slightest smile across my lips. So slight that I didn't even realize I was doing it until I noticed my reflection in the metal napkin dispenser.

I skimmed the menu carefully, not wanting to draw a blank the way I did last night when we went to that dingy diner. My eyes paused at the familiar entrées.

"Lamb stew" I whispered to myself.

"Huh?" I looked up and shook my head not realizing that I said it aloud.

"Sorry, I just remembered Char-" I stopped myself and bit my lip.

"Go on."

"Uh no, I shouldn't."

"Charlotte?" He asked.

"Yes, she made me it for the first time last month." I cleared my throat and closed my menu. "It-it was good."

"So order it." Donovan insisted.

"I couldn't. I don't like-memories." I folded my hands in my lap. Donovan nodded, setting aside his menu as our glasses were filled with ice water by the waiter.

"I've seen you at Lush."

"You have?" I tilted my head.

"You ran out of a room. Passed right by me before I warned Greene."

"You warned him?"

"Two days before we killed him. He was in there because he was hiding from me. I thought I'd surprise him that night." Donovan chuckled. "I didn't remember you until last night when you looked me in my eyes." He leaned forward on his elbows, looking right at me.

I already knew which night he was referring to, but I was now distracted by his glare into my soul. As if he were trying to figure something out about me.

"I'm sorry that I ran."

"I don't need you to be sorry." He shook his head. "I need you to stop doing it."

I glanced down at my palms and sighed. I felt bad for doing it, especially since now I had bandages on my hands and my body was in minor pain.

"I told you, I don't like memories."

"Running away isn't a memory."

"It is for me." I admitted. "I'm trapped with another man that hates me. It's the only way out." I could tell that Donovan was confused by this. He knew I meant Greene but he didn't know about my foster father. All the men I encountered hated me so I ran.

"It's not the only way out." Donovan sat back in the booth. "You're free to go Rosemary." He waved toward the door, testing me. Or was he? He was the type that didn't need to test people. He was so direct that it was hard to keep up.

"But I'm not."

"If you're smart, you won't." He warned. I looked past him through the window and noticed two well dressed figures step out of a black car.

"I won't." I narrowed my eyes and then pointed behind Donovan. He followed my finger, then turned back with a placid expression. Maybe the men gave me anxiety but it didn't seem to concern him.

In that moment, the waiter arrived.

"Good afternoon, what will you both be having?"

"We need five minutes." Donovan demanded, handing over our menus. The waiter nodded and walked away.

Donovan stood up. "C'mon." He kept his eyes on the door as he took my arm and pulled me along.

The men entered right as Donovan pushed open the door to the mens bathroom.

"Do you know them?" He asked me, his tone calm.

"No, I just-didn't trust the way they looked." I admitted. Dark cars and suits scared me especially after Nate and Lance barged in to murder Greene. "Who are they?"

"They're the reason why we had to leave New York."

"How do they know we're here?"

"I don't know what they know Rose-" he stopped mid-sentence and narrowed his eyes. Within a split second, he wrapped his arm around my waist and pulled me into a stall, shutting the door and lifting me to sit on the back of the toilet.

The door of the bathroom opened and two sets of footsteps sounded. My breathing slowed but my heart raced at the possibility of being found. Though Donovan seemed calm, I knew that he was silently cursing in his head.

"We've been here for three hours and no sign of him or the girl." One of the men with baritone voice said.

"Either we got a fake tip or they know we're looking." The other man replied.

"They probably know." Baritone laughed. "After all, we took the chef girl."

I bit my bottom lip and looked at Donovan to keep myself calm. However, upon looking at him and feeling his warm hand on my thighs, the taboo thoughts that I had buried earlier resurfaced.

I must've looked too long because Donovan turned to me and looked right at my lip stick halfway in my mouth. I returned his gaze and felt his hands move up my leg slowly then back down.

I took a silent deep breath that he noticed, which motivated him to continue. So he moved his hands upward to my waist and then his hand disappeared under my shirt, moving upward from my stomach.

I almost moaned but Donovan shook his head as a warning. It was a subtle gesture that caused my body to react and moisten. Sexual touches in a bathroom while hiding in plain sight. It was something out of an erotic novel!

His soft fingers grazed my breasts and pulled at my nipples willing me to moan but I bit down harder on my lip to suppress it. I didn't want to be the one to get us caught. Especially as I was writhing and biting like a horny nympho.

Donovan's lips found my cheek and he kissed it, creating a slow trail down that ended at my lips. I welcomed his without hesitation as his hands continued to explore my tender crevices.

"I'll call Ashton and let him know the situation." The two men turned the sink off and then their steps gradually faded as the door shut close on their way out.

But with lips in contact and body temperatures on high, neither of us noticed. Or maybe we did, but we didn't care.

Donovan lifted me up and pushed my back to the stall door.

"They almost heard you." He grunted, squeezing my ass and biting my neck. I squealed in pleasure.

"I'm sorry." I moaned, running my fingers through his silky hair. It had been just like my day dream. Only now this was really happening and I was sure of it because my ass had been pinched a few times so I wasn't dreaming. Donovan Faust has me pushed against a wall as if there was an irresistible connection between us both that caused crazed sexual tension. I felt honored to have his lips caressing my neck and his fingers massaging my tender nipples.

Suddenly, Donovan slowed his hungry actions and paced his breath by setting me down but keeping his face close to mine. I almost begged him for more but I couldn't grow weak to him the way I'd grown weak to other things in life. So I allowed the only noise to come from our labored breathing.

I attempted to turn and leave the stall after a few seconds but Donovan pulled the fabric of my shirt with force so that I was closer to him.

"When you listen you're such a good girl." He said right in my ear. I nearly shivered from the soft spoken words.

"I'll try it more often." I didn't mean those words to be sexual but when heard him let out a sigh I knew that my obedience turned him on.

Donovan unlocked the stall and nudged me out.

"There's a window in the last stall." He said. "We'll leave through there."

• • • • • •

It was a rare occurrence, me inside of a sex room at Lush. Greene was glaring down at me, keeping a beer bottle close to his lips.

It was our third meeting since the contract and each had gotten progressively worse. I no longer knew what to expect from such a gruesome man but the only thing that kept me sane was knowing that intercourse was not part of the deal.

However, that didn't mean that I wasn't terrified. He had the key to my life story and I had to work for it.

"I have a treat for you." He smirked.

"I don't want it."

"I bet you do."

"Why're we up here?" I asked partly as a way to run out the clock. We usually did this in a hotel or at his apartment for an hour.

"Because I'm avoiding a-friend." He placed the bottle down. "Show me what's under that." He pointed to my denim romper and I sighed.

"I-don't want to." Greene narrowed his eyes at me then in a split moment grabbed my neck and squeezed.

"You signed the contract bitch." He said between clenched teeth. I gasped from his hold blocking my airways and grabbed at him before he let go with a hard shove.

I stumbled back to the door and heaved from the pressure around my neck. Greene was an animal, the worst kind of man there was.

"If you create any more issues from this point forward I'll make sure you never-"

"Greene!" There was a knock at the door and I recognized the voice of one of the security guards. "You have a visitor." Greene's pupils dilated and he cursed under his breath.

"Who?"

"You know who Greene." A different voice said.

"Help me!" I yelled without a second thought. Before Greene could get to me, the door swung open and two men stood in the front. I blew right past them and headed to the safety of the dressing room.

With my current knowledge I knew that it had been Donovan who was the "visitor". He'd been there in a black three piece suit and took a slight step to the side when I rushed out. He had seen me at Lush, running away as usual.

• • • • • •

Donovan held his arms out for me to jump into so that I could land safely out of the bathroom window. I almost lost my balance on the way down but he stabilized me.

"Does Phil know we're back here?" I asked.

Donovan took out his phone.

"Yeah, but those guys inside were following something familiar since they were tipped off. I'm guessing the car."

"Is that what they said?" He moved only his eyes from the phone screen to look at me.

"Didn't you hear them say that?"

"Oh uh-no I was- my mind was-" I stopped as Donovan let out a short chuckle. They'd clearly said it while my panties were soaked from Donovan's touch.

"Phil is going to get rid of the car then grab another one and meet us ahead."

"What does that mean?"

"It means," He shrugged off his navy suit jacket, "We should start walking." He placed the jacket over my shoulders as the rain continued to drizzle on us.

Chapter Eighteen: Business and Pleasure

The first ten minutes of walking were filled with the sound of our shoes crunching autumn leaves and rain droplets landing gently on the sturdy trees.

I kept Donovan's suit jacket wrapped around my shoulders, occasionally inhaling the unique cologne that generously coated the fibers of the tailored piece. It was a scent that I'd never had the pleasure of smelling until meeting Donovan. It wasn't part of a memory, it was fresh and new.

"What changed?" I asked after the eleventh minute of uncomfortable silence.

I asked hoping that he would understand the context. Just last night he'd hinted that the situation would be less stressful without me. He even displayed his frustration after I took a deep midnight dive to escape. Now, he was lending me a soft jacket and guiding me to safety. It seemed temporary and I didn't want to expect kindness all of a sudden.

"I actually enjoy silence Rosemary." He responded.

"Is that why you have that lake house?"

"No, I have that lake house to bring acquaintances to when I'm around here."

I scoffed at his response, louder than expected.

"Must be a female haven."

"Not exactly." He checked his watch. "Acquaintances also consist of some business partners."

"The men I had to serve drinks to?" I glanced up at him and watched his lips curve at the corner.

"You're a Lush girl, you like serving men." He stated.

I pressed my lips together, holding back a response that would be considered disrespectful. It was a common assumption that Lush gurls enjoyed serving men. Conveniently, the main people who assumed this were the men that were served.

"Serving and Servicing are two different things." I said matter-of-factly.

"You enjoy both."

"I enjoy neither." I rolled my eyes. "Have you been served at Lush?"

"I don't mix business and pleasure."

"Maybe you haven't had the right type of pleasure." I said in a sing-song tone.

Donovan took my arm, making us stop in our tracks.

"What do you know about the right type of pleasure?" He looked down at me with a straight face.

"I know that we're told to mix business with pleasure because that's what our clients want but won't say that they want." I shrugged.

It was true, business men loved saying they keep the two separate but get them in a dim room with three shots of tequila and they want nothing more than to talk about their achievements, ventures, and accolades.

"Really?" He folded his arms. "How?"

"How do we mix the two?" I considered his question. "Well the business they're in usually dictates how we approach them."

"For example..." He said, waiting for me to continue.

"I guess-well say I'm approaching someone like you- a crim-a gang-um-" I gulped while looking at Donovan who had his brows raised in anticipation for what I would refer to him as.

I was stuck since in my head I could call him a criminal but aloud it sounded too dismissive and blasphemous. He was organized and efficient. So what was that?

"Someone like me." He said as a way to end my speculation.

"Yes, someone like-you." I let out a nervous laugh then continued. "Based on how you dress and carry yourself it's clear that you're very important." I shrugged. "But of course that means I wouldn't be able to claim you as a client."

"But a Lush class girl would?"

"How do you know about that rule?"

"I like to know everything about the business I get into." He motioned for us to continue walking. "But clearly I didn't know as much as I thought since Greene was there terrorizing you all."

I didn't really want to think about Greene right now. I actually never wanted to think about him but with the way that Donovan was actually speaking to me as a person, I wanted all negativity out of my head.

"You said you don't mix business with pleasure?" I narrowed my eyes. "So why were you sleeping with your chef?"

Donovan actually chuckled and shook his head. "I met Grace when I was negotiating a property deal with her father, he's an important figure in a city nearby. Like most women, she didn't know the extent of my work so my business and pleasure never intersected."

"Do you really believe that?" I asked.

He locked my eyes with his and in that moment I felt a tenderness in him. It was the first vulnerable exchange we'd had together and no words were necessary. Just the soft burn of curious eyes as thin fog coated the air. He hadn't expected me to ask that and quite frankly, neither had I. But it seemed to sand down his ridges as he considered.

"Not anymore." He said softly.

Just as I started to get comfortable in the calm mood, Donovan tore away from our trance and gazed upward with a squint.

"What's up the hill?"

"Phil." He took my hand to guide me up a steep area, then came beside me.

I squeezed the jacket tighter but was reminded of something that had not been addressed as we ventured up. I sighed and looked over at him.

"Can you please tell me now?" I wanted to know what had changed between us where he now felt it necessary to talk to me, and kiss me, and be a bit more patient with me.

Donovan sighed as well.

"You know," drops of rain were coming down harder after a few minutes of clearance, "this is the most I've heard you talk Rosemary."

At first, my face fell at his statement because I realized that he didn't take my question seriously.

But then I noticed a chuckle come from him as he removed the jacket from my shoulder and held it over my head so that I wouldn't get too wet from the rain.

I smiled in return, appreciative of the uncharacteristic gesture.

"C'mon, Phil's right up there." Donovan said as we finished the up hill walk to meet Phil in a new white Cadillac.

Chapter Nineteen: Change of Heart

That evening Hannah, Nate, and Lance had to return to the lake house due to the information they'd received about Ashton's men at the restaurant.

So we all ate dinner at the table and discussed the business surrounding Ashton. Well, they discussed, I sat quietly taking tiny scoops of mashed potatoes onto my fork.

"We'll have to stay here for a while." Nate said after they'd been notified of the proximity of Ashton's men to us.

"You and Lance will. Hannah you'll head back to the city with Rosemary." Donovan said.

Now I looked up from my plate because he was going to relocate me again. The city didn't mean "back home" it meant to some obscure place that I would be watched like a hawk at.

Hannah cleared her throat before muttering, "I'm not sure how that would help."

Donovan's expression was unchanging but he looked right at Hannah, sitting further back in his chair.

"Is there something you really want to say?" He tested.

Hannah looked around the table at all the eyes that were focused on her. Even I was taken by surprise because I didn't have the gall to speak up to Donovan.

Hannah stood up with her plate, pushing her seat so far back that it almost tipped over.

"No Donovan." She took Nate's plate as well then went into the kitchen.

I quickly grabbed my plate, Lance's, and Donovan's then hurried to follow behind her.

"I wasn't even done." I heard Lance say as I disappeared into the kitchen. I was supposed to do all the cleanup but Hannah clearly needed to get away from the men at the table. So I placed the plates in the sink and let her scrub away under the hot water.

"He thinks he's protecting us by sending us to the city." She said in a low tone since we were close to the dining room. "But we wouldn't be safe. We'd be under permanent lockdown while they drown those guys in the lake." She shook her head.

I leaned on the counter beside the sink, continuing to listen.

"I love working for him but sometimes-" she turned to look at me, "sometimes he only cares about his own decisions and not how they impact others." She sighed.

Again, all I could do was listen to her. I liked to think that I was a good listener at the very least.

"I'm sorry, I shouldn't be venting to you."

I shrugged, not wanting to discourage her from continuing it from the possibility of it happening again. Hannah knew Donovan better than I ever would and it was clear that this situation was unique for everyone.

"How was the doctor's visit?" She asked to change the subject.

"Um-it was-okay." I lifted my arm up to show her. She gave me a tight smile.

"I'm glad you're okay. I asked Donovan to go easy on you today. He was really upset last night but he just doesn't understand where Lush girls really come from especially with impulsive decisions."

That answered one of my questions of the day. I was impressed that Hannah really had the power to make Donovan treat me slightly better. Even if it was only for a day. It mattered.

"He was pretty nice today. I wasn't sure why." I heard Hannah chuckle but continued. "I hope it carries to-"

"Rosemary, Donovan wants you upstairs." Nate came in and reported.

I nodded and went to leave the kitchen, but Nate caught my arm. "Don't go running away tonight. I'd like to sleep peacefully. Got it?" He was firm in his words so I nodded again and then shook free of his grip.

Nate wasn't joking. I was sure he'd been up for almost twenty three hours straight so that had to be part of his hostility.

Donovan was in his office when I got upstairs. I entered and shut the door behind me quickly. Stone always found a way near me so the quicker I acted, the better.

"I want you-" he looked up from the laptop he was on, "to ask me what you want to know." He was propped against his desk casually.

"Huh?"

"You want to know so much. So ask."

"But I thought you weren't willing to answer my questions."

"I had a change of heart." He pointed to the leather sofa by the wall. "Sit." I obeyed, partly because my feet still hurt from walking so much earlier and I was happy to oblige.

"Why am I here?" I asked.

Donovan set the laptop down and pushed off of the desk, straightening his blue tie.

"You're here with me to be kept safe from some issue that arose last week." He answered.

I'd figured Donovan was sheltering me when he hid me in the stall. If he wanted me dead he would've left me in the booth or let me run away when I thought I had the chance.

"What issue?"

"An issue." He repeated. So this would be a selective question and answer session.

"Do you plan on killing anyone because of this issue?"

Donovan shrugged, "We'll see."

I shook my head and was tempted to walk out without another word until I thought about one last question.

"Why were you nicer to me today?"

"Thank Hannah. She's more like you than I thought." I smirked. I'd known the answer but I knew that I'd feel more complete hearing it from Donovan especially after such a progressive day.

I didn't want to ask any more questions. Something told me that knowing more would be worse than knowing less. Especially in this situation.

I slowly stood from the leather chair.

"Do you mind if I go to bed now?" I asked.

Donovan tilted his head.

"No more?"

"I don't think so." He studied my face intently.

"Then it's my turn." He started which caught me off guard. "Why did you yell for help that night at Lush?" His voice was soft but my heart began to pound from the pressure of such a question.

"I-I didn't want to be alone in a room with Greene. Ever." I responded quite plainly.

"Why?"

"I hated him."

"Because?"

"Because-" I paused and bit my lip, terrified to speak further about this. He was pressing a wound and he knew it. "Because he-he hurt me and-"

"And because he had something over you." Donovan said.

I looked up and gaped. He reached over the desk and produced a manila folder.

I stared between him and the flimsy material. How did he know about Greene having something over me?

"This is yours. Nate and Lance found it in Greene's apartment. No one has opened it." He held it out to me.

I didn't know what to say. Was that my birth certificate and foster record? The identity that Greene held from me. They'd found it and now Donovan was giving it back to me. He didn't have to. He could easily do what Greene had done and leverage his powerful position to make me work for it in whatever way he saw fit. But no, he was freely returning it to me. Most importantly, he was returning it to me without a catch.

My eyes met Donovan's for final confirmation before I pinched the folder and gained control. I wanted to hug it, and him, but I didn't.

"How did you know?"

"There was a contract." Donovan made a hand gesture to imply that it was displayed on a wall which didn't surprise me because Greene always had it on display like some award.

"Thank you for this." I finally thanked him genuinely for something.

Donovan gave a short nod then looked at his watch.

"Make sure you shut the door please." He ordered and I was never happier to comply and leave his presence.

CHAPTER TWENTY: CONTROL ME

The manila folder sat on top of the bed for an hour. I didn't touch it. I didn't open it. I just looked at it and wondered what could possibly be inside.

What happened to my real parents? What was my real last name? Where was I from?

I wanted the answer to these questions but I didn't know if I was ready to find out the answers now. Especially because of where I was and my lack of freedom.

So I walked to the dresser by the closet and slipped the folder into the top drawer. It would be out of sight and I could approach it with a more level head if I wasn't forced to look at it all night. But as I showered and crawled into bed, it stayed on my mind. Even when I tried to think about something, anything, else the thought returned.

I didn't want to be left alone with my own thoughts. They were dangerous and often toxic.

I stood up from the bed, figuring that I'd go to Hannah and talk to her if she was awake. She would understand my uneasy feeling.

The hallway was dark and it took a moment for my eyes to adjust to the absence of light.

However, as I started down the hall, I noticed a thin stream of light filter out from one room. Nate's figure was illuminated, still dressed in his suit from earlier without the jacket.

I stood aside, my back pressed to a door. I knew he couldn't see me but I figured that I didn't want to take any chances. Donovan highly disliked me but Nate hated me.

He crossed to the door opposite his and gave a single knock with his knuckle against the wood. Not even a second later, Hannah answered with her body wrapped in a deep purple satin robe and her hair tied in a low ponytail.

"You still mad at me?" He asked her, leaning on the door frame and reaching for her hand. She pulled away.

"Yes, you should've said something." Hannah protested.

Nate scoffed.

"It's done Hannah. You'll be safe in New York and that's all that matters to me." He went to reach for her hand again. This time she didn't resist.

"If Ashton finds Rosemary, this entire operation is over. We'd all face time, even you." He said.

What did that even mean? If Ashton found me then Donovan's syndicate would suffer. I knew absolutely nothing so how did the fate of their freedom come down to me? I didn't know how that was possible but perhaps that was what Donovan was alluding to when he wouldn't explain the issue that resulted in this hiding.

Hannah nodded. "I know. I just don't want us all to be split up." She shrugged.

"Can you let me in now?" Nate asked.

Hannah sighed then stepped aside so that he could enter. He smirked and loosened his tie before ultimately disappearing inside.

I assumed going to Hannah to talk about my issue was out of the question now that she was preoccupied. So I would have to stay in the room by myself with that folder taunting me to open it. But even if it did happen and I figured out my truth, I was still trapped here with nowhere to go and the reality that I had some type of value because if Ashton got his hands on me, something bade would happened to everyone else.

"What're you doing Rosemary?" I heard Donovan's voice and jumped into the air.

He was shutting the double doors to his study across from where I stood.

"Oh-um-I couldn't sleep."

Donovan approached me and stood right in front of me.

I looked up at him wondering why he chose to be so direct at this moment. He could easily walk to his room and pretend that I didn't exist. Or he could just ignore my confusion as he often had. Instead he stood in front of me, staring down.

"Do you mind?"

"Do I mind what?" Was he coming onto me again? I was always so confused by him. But I was flattered because this time I would play along.

"You're leaning on my door Rosemary." He said with a bit of humor in his tone.

I turned over my shoulder and noticed that I did in fact have my body resting on a whole door.

I let out a nervous chuckle, embarrassed that I'd thought in this moment he had wanted to seduce me. Who did I think he was? If the lights had been on in this grand hallway then he surely would've seen the blush across my cheeks.

"Oh, I'm sorry." I quickly stepped aside.

Donovan opened his door then looked over his shoulder at me. "You coming in?"

"What?"

"You said you can't sleep. C'mon." I didn't hesitate to follow him inside the all too familiar master bedroom.

However, I almost ran out when I saw Stone asleep right beside the window seat. I moved slowly to the opposite side of the room, completely disregarding Donovan's eyes on me.

"You know he's not going to attack you right?"

"He might."

"He won't." Donovan rolled his sleeves up as he walked to the mini bar.

"Why is he in here?" He usually stayed with Phil downstairs.

"I guess he just wandered in." Donovan poured liquid into two glasses while he spoke. "You can sit."

I nodded and slowly made my way to the edge of the bed, keeping my eyes on the dog.

Donovan handed me a glass and then went on to detach his suspenders.

"What's this?" I sniffed the glass of clear yellowish-white liquid.

"Something to help you sleep." I stared into the glass and hesitantly took a sip surprised that the taste was slightly sweet and not too strong.

"Is this what you drink when you have trouble sleeping?"

"I don't have trouble going to sleep." He said as if it were common sense to me.

"Not even when you-" I stopped myself right on time. Before I could say something that was too bold.

But my abrupt pause alerted Donovan. He stopped undressing and narrowed his eyes.

"When I?"

"Nothing. I shouldn't ask about negative things. This is good by the way." I showed him the glass that he had poured.

Donovan chuckled.

"When I what Rosemary?" He took the glass from my hand and tilted my chin up to look at him. "When I torture people?" I tried to look away but his fingers were firm and he kept my head focused. "When I murder people? Is that what you were going to say?"

"Yes." I said, gulping hard. I couldn't even sugar coat my original question. I could never bring myself to do any of those things and knew that I would never be able to sleep after that type of experience.

"No, I don't have trouble sleeping after torturing and murdering." He handed the glass back to me and then stepped away.

"Why?" I felt inclined to ask once I was in control of my head again.

"For one, I no longer get my hands dirty." He was the head of the syndicate. Of course he didn't. "But when I did, the people deserved what they got."

"No one deserves to die." I said. Donovan lifted an eyebrow at me.

"Is that what you think?" I shrugged. I'd always heard that said so I figured it was true.

"It's what I like to think."

"Don't be so gulliable." Donovan crossed his arms, "Greene might've been a bad client but he wasn't the worst type of man we've bumped."

It was hard for me to consider a more horrible man than Greene and it was harder for me to imagine a more gory death scenario.

"Why do you do it?" I asked what I assumed was a very simple question. Donovan studied me for several seconds then met my eyes and smirked.

"Because I'm good at it." He winked at me then went over to the closet.

I wasn't sure if I was more scared at his answer or more scared at what lay behind his answer. He was good at murdering and torturing? He hired people who were good at both too. Lush was bad but the world outside of it was even worse. Especially with men like Donovan choosing your final resting place.

I must've contemplated what I was more scared of for several minutes because when I finally escaped my daze, Donovan was undressed with his bare chest and lounge pants on display for me. I quickly looked away and set my empty glass down. An attractive man was still foreign to me. I was barely comfortable in his presence while he wore a suit. Half naked was a bit much.

"Feeling sleepy?"

"Yeah, and-light headed." My body was heating up from the quick sight and as much as I didn't want to be left alone tonight, I knew that I should leave Donovan's presence before I buckled to my knees and let him do what he pleased to me."I should-um-I should-"

"You can stay in here if-"

"No, I should go." I stood up.

"To be stuck in your own head from that folder." He said.

I turned to Donovan who was looking at me from the bathroom mirror.

"How did you know?" I asked, walking to the door of the master bath.

"Hannah." Was all he needed to say for me to understand. Hannah knew what a loss of identity meant.

I sighed, knowing I couldn't be alone tonight, and went to the side of the bed. Darkness enveloped the room as soon as my body wrapped into the satin sheets. Donovan came over to the bed shortly after.

It was odd, sleeping beside a semi-naked man that had the capacity to order a hit on me at any moment. Up until today, I hadn't been able to see past his handsome though dangerous demeanor. Now I knew danger radiated from his aura but he was slightly redeemed by the existence of a personality beyond the cold one that I'd been shown.

"Donovan?" I whispered, rolling over to face him.

His arm was over his eyes but he spoke.

"Yes?"

"Thank you." I said softly. He didn't have to help me tonight but he was doing it so it felt right to thank him.

Donovan's arm lifted from his eyes and he turned to meet my eyes. Despite the absolute darkness, I could make out those green eyes.

"Go to sleep Rosemary." He whispered, but his eyes didn't leave mine.

For whatever reason our gazes held, and my heart beat became irregular.

I could feel the heat from earlier making a comeback and traveling further down my body. It was only a look, but it reminded me of when we were in the stall together. All it took was that look and my sex began to react. Then, some bold bone in my body prompted me to lean over and place my lips close to his without them touching.

"Is this what you want?" He asked in such a low tone that the subtle hum sent a shiver down my spine and made me let out a gasp before planting my lips onto his.

There was a sense of urgency in the way that he responded to my lips. His hands wrapped around my waist, pulling me on top of him as the kiss intensified. I didn't know what had gotten into me but I couldn't control my lustful response to Donovan.

The feeling of his hands on my back was a comfort that I'd never felt from a man before. His lips presented a form of comfort and a level of aggression that even my most masochistic client could not obtain with such ease.

I straddled him and pulled away from his soft lips slowly.

"It is." I said, starting a trail of kisses down his chest to his waistline.

Donovan licked his lips and caught my arm just as my fingers pinched his briefs.

"You don't know what you're doing." He warned. But I ignored him, feeling a new sense of independence as I had initiated a heated sexual session and was revived by a real man. Not a sappy Lush client.

His dick was exposed as a rod of perfection that Lush girls could only dream about in the dressing room. It was a popular topic of discussion especially since Lush class girls fucked their clients and were always prepared to gossip about penis sizes and shapes.

But this one; never had I seen an erect member so deserving of being licked, sucked, and gagged on. If I'd thought he was intriguing before, well now-now I had to taste a masterpiece.

My mouth engulfed him the way his satin sheets had engulfed me when I slid into his bed. Fingers laced through my hair and pulled, reestablishing control of our situation. I gagged when his hips lifted upward which caused Donovan to throw his head back. He repeated the gesture until a tear strolled down my cheek. I couldn't recall a time when the act of oral pleasure was thrilling to me.

My head bobbed while I struggled to take all of him in.

"Ahh, Rose." I heard him say, mid grunt then he pulled my hair up to remove me from him. Donovan sat up and wiped my bottom lip with his thumb gently.

I didn't want to be pulled off from the fullness this soon. But he was clearly the one who called the shots, so I had to obey.

He pulled me up closer to him on the bed and then our position was swiftly shifted as he hovered over my body. In a single motion, Donovan pulled my shorts down with my panties and bent to kiss my neck. I moaned in anticipation and writhed from the damp feeling between my legs.

Donovan gripped my thighs and pushed them up, glancing down at the shine that he created between my legs. I was almost embarrassed at being easily aroused. However, I'd never been pleased in this way and my body was in shock so I had to listen.

Donovan used the tip of his finger to rub it up and down my slit.

"Mmm." I gripped the sheets.

"Has your pussy been touched before?" Donovan asked.

I bit my lip and nodded shamefully.

"Oh really?" He questioned, not disappointed but amused. "How many times?"

"Mmm" I reacted again to the pressure his thumb put on my clit. "Only-only a couple times."

Donovan lowered himself between my legs and pushed my thighs further apart. His warmth was so close that I felt orgasmic by indirect touch.

"It's been touched, but has it been-"

"No!" I answered, squirming. That definitely had never happened.

I took a deep breath to contain the moan that I was prepared to let out as I felt his lips close to mine. I knew I was close and it sucked because nothing had even happened. But as soon as the softness of his tongue touched my sensitive core and the warmth of his mouth tickled my flesh, I knew I had nothing left in me. I couldn't keep it together for very long and it was proven the moment he eventually flicked my clit. Before I knew it, I was releasing myself and pulling at the sheets on the bed. His hand gripped my neck as I finished riding out the orgasm.

"So sweet." He said, biting his bottom lip.

I blushed and sighed, touching his arm so that I could hold onto something.

Donovan moved upward to his position in the bed and laid his head back.

"I want more." I said hungrily, touching his chest. Donovan moved my hand aside.

"It's late. Lay down."

"But I want more."

"No you don't." He corrected me.

"I'm not a child Donovan. I know what I want." I declared almost angrily.

"Don't do this Rosemary."

"Don't do what? Tell you the truth." I watched Donovan's body lift up a bit to look at me.

"You're distracted and emotional." He shook his head. "So sleep it off."

"You made me 'distracted and emotional'!" I got out of the bed. "Why would you do all that and then act as if I'm irrational?" I was fuming.

Donovan looked at me for longer than I was comfortable with and then he stripped the sheets off of himself and got out the bed as well.

"I'm doing you a favor." He pointed to both of our bodies while he came around the bed to the side I was on. "It's a bad idea."

I glared at him, my breathing was hard and steady. It was the most emotion I had evoked in his presence and I didn't even know how he was handling this new side.

"It wasn't a bad idea ten minutes ago."

"Ten minutes ago, you were only sucking my dick." He pointed out. "Now, you're talking too fucking much. So go to sleep." His tone was calm and stern for a man that had just dropped every curse word in the book.

I stared back at him, upset with no way to express it. I hated him all over again. He was toying with me and deceiving me.

"You can't control me."

"You sure about that?" He narrowed his eyes down at me. I tried to do the same but evidently my body complied and I sunk down to the bed slowly. I wasn't sure about it, or anything else in my life for that matter.

Donovan stayed for only a beat longer then pulled open the door to leave the bedroom.

Chapter Twenty One: Not Sorry

My eyes slowly opened when I felt something lick my hand. I made out the figure after my second giggle and jolted at the sight of Stone. He was seated, staring at me, and waging his tail. I was surprised he hadn't mauled me in my sleep like the ferocious beast he seemed to be.

I looked to the opposite side of the bed and noticed it was empty. Donovan, and everyone else for that matter, had probably gotten ready for the eventful day while I was recovering from the most confusing night of my life. Actually, second place to the night Greene was murdered.

I went back to my room so that I could take a shower and change my clothes. Hannah and I were being forced back to the city so the least I could do was look presentable to take the long trip back.

When I finally made my way downstairs there was a breakfast buffet spread out on the dining table. It was an elaborate display of muffins, pancakes, turkey bacon, sausage, and fruit. Honestly, I'd been fed well under Donovan which wasn't always the case in my non captive life. Roth only liked skinny girls at Lush. It wasn't up for debate or negotiation.

When I reached for a muffin, a woman stepped out of the kitchen with a pitcher of orange juice in hand and smiled when she saw me look up, mid grab.

"Good morning Rosemary!" Her voice was high pitched and sounded oddly enthusiastic considering the fact that she was only greeting me and not the Queen of England.

"Do I know you?"

"You don't." She set down the pitcher then flicked some blonde hair over her shoulder before shaking my hand. "I'm taking Grace's place here until everything calms down." Taking Grace's place? So Donovan called in some new girl to keep him sexual company since Grace was MIA and I was being sent off.

I hated myself for even allowing him to have emotional control over me. For a few hours yesterday my heart had been growing tender for him and now here I was as his disposable captive.

I looked out the window that faced the lake and noticed Donovan, Lance, and two unfamiliar men in suits discussing something. The slight breeze blew his otherwise perfect hair just enough for him to run his fingers through it. Yesterday, I would easily have considered the gesture to be sexy, but this morning it just made me scoff and look away.

"Isn't he handsome?" The woman I had just met gushed, looking out the window as well.

"How do you know him?" I asked, avoiding her question.

"I was a pastry chef at The Coral Club." She leaned on the table. "He liked the cheesecake and asked to meet me. Next thing you know, he took me back to-"

"Okay," I looked at her with my brows furrowed. "I get it." It was confirmed now that they'd been involved and thus I wanted nothing to do with Donovan.

"Good, you met Pharrah." Hannah entered the dining room with an iPad in hand. It was comforting to see her.

Pharrah gave us a tight smile and then disappeared into the kitchen. Hannah rolled her eyes and walked closer to me.

"Was she bothering you?"

"No, not at all. She's very-bubbly." Was the best way I could describe her since I didn't come in contact with naturally perky women often.

"She thinks she's going to marry Donovan. I guess the fact that he brings her out in public is deceiving." My face might have given up the fact that I hated knowing this information. This girl would be alone with him in the house and they already had an intimate relationship.

"Maybe he shouldn't lead people on." I suggested. Hannah shrugged, none the wiser.

"Smells amazing in here!" Lance exclaimed, as all three men walked inside through the back door. He reached for a strip of bacon. "Pharrah, you know how to make magic."

She stepped out of the kitchen with a grin and approached the men.

"It's my job." She touched Donovan's arm and leaned up to peck his lips. He cocked an eyebrow at her action then turned to look at the table, his cheeks a faint shade of pink.

"Where's Nate?"

"On a call with the guys in New York. He's ensuring that we have a system in place to confirm that Rose and I are safe when we arrive back in the city." Hannah said.

"Sorry that you two have to be sent back." Lance claimed through a mouth full of corn muffin.

"Truly." Donovan followed up, looking at Hannah and I while he poured a cup of coffee.

"You're not sorry." I scoffed in what I assumed was a whisper. However, Hannah's attention snapped to me and I watched as Donovan slowly set down the coffee pot while focusing on me. I gulped at his hard gaze but crossed my arms over my chest regardless.

"What was that?" Donovan asked.

"I didn't say anything." I lied and Donovan knew it because he grabbed my arm and took me down the hall until we were in some room off of the library.

He released my arm with a shove after he shut the French doors.

"That hurt!" I exaggerated, rubbing my arm.

"I don't care."

"I'm not surprised." I fired back. Donovan rolled his eyes and then set his mug down. My heart was racing and I felt my hands shake. "You're such an asshole." I finally said to him, feeling tears escape my eyes.

"Am I?" He asked sarcastically.

"You just had to bring that girl here and get rid of me. You held me here and now you're throwing me away like you don't care at all. So yes, you're a horrible man and an asshole." I confessed. Maybe I was beginning to like him but it went beyond that. I was tired of this feeling of emptiness. The feeling of anxiety that I would never be around for long enough.

Donovan kept his eyes on me and his hands in the pockets of his gray slacks.

"I know that," he began, "everyone out there knows that," he pointed over his shoulder. "But you-you're just now finding out." His tone was blunt as he shook his head in disbelief.

I couldn't control the gradual water works that had the nerve to come out at this moment.

Donovan removed the kerchief from his waistcoat pocket and held it out for me. "When you're done come outside. I'll have Hannah pack your stuff." Then he turned to once again, leave me.

• • • • • •

I eventually willed myself to spare the hysterics, not wanting to think any further about the man who forced me into this situation. All I wanted was to get into the car and be far away from this place.

In front of the house were three black Range Rovers with Hannah standing beside one. She followed my movement as I walked toward her.

"Are you okay?"

"I will be." I shrugged.

Hannah didn't pry, she gave a tight smile and then called Nate over to brief me on what was to happen.

"You're riding in a separate car to prevent anyone from targeting you. Each car has a driver and an armed guard. Don't ask them questions. Don't try and jump out the car. Don't run away." Nate emphasized each point. "If anything happens, press the alarm under your seat. It alerts us here and the headquarters in the city." I nodded. "Once you're back, Hannah will bring you to the apartment where you'll stay until we give her the okay. Don't give her a hard time. Okay?" He finished.

Hannah scoffed and opened the back door of the last vehicle for me.

"You've never given me a hard time Rosemary. Don't mind him." She said with Nate still beside her.

I actually didn't mind him since it was what I expected. A surprise would be him speaking to me kindly but that wasn't going to happen.

I ducked into the car next to a large man who was tucking a handgun into his breast strap. We made eye contact and he broke it by flashing me a grin and then flicking his blazer closed.

Donovan came out of the house with Pharrah following seconds behind. He held his hand out for her to stay at the door step while he went straight to Nate and pointed to the first Range Rover. I squeezed the kerchief he had given me and glanced at the man next to me again.

"Can you get the folder from my bag please?" Maybe I could summon the courage to open it on the long ride to Manhattan because it would distract me easily.

"You're good!" Nate called, giving a thumbs up to the drivers.

The car Hannah was in pulled away first, followed by the decoy, and then the car I was in.

Although I really wanted to, I didn't turn around. Not even to look at Donovan for what might be the last time for a long time. I was accustom to this. Leaving someone or a family in a large vehicle. It was always easier to not look back at anyone. Especially when you knew that they never cared in the first place.

Chapter Twenty Two: Dead Woman Walking

I stared out the window of the moving car and sighed as we rolled past rows of brick structures and iridescent street lamps.

A hand on my exposed thigh prompted a switch in glance that alerted my captor.

"You've gained weight." Greene chuckled to himself and gave my thigh a squeeze. I shook my head, knowing good and well that Greene didn't know me well enough to notice weight gain. He simply said anything to disrespect me.

"Must be from all the dick you're taking. Isn't that what they say?"

"Who's 'they'?" I didn't really care, but I hated these rides back to his apartment or to various hotels. They were awkward and I generally spent them contemplating my life choices.

"I don't know but it's true." He claimed.

I moved his hand from my thigh and peered back out the window. We were going past the St. Regis Hotel and that seemed odd to me, especially since it was a Sunday night and he usually checked us in for our escapades.

"You passed the hotel."

"I know. We need to make a stop." Greene said without his usual cocky grin. In fact, his delivery threw me off so much that I looked at him until the car finally came to a stop at a building along Riverside Drive.

A lanky man slid into the back seat of the car without a word. I turned to try and makeout his face but a dark shadow was cast over half of it. What was this? A taxi service now?

"Cinnamon, come out the car for a minute." Greene ushered me to follow him out. Furrowing my brows, I followed him to the side walk a few feet from the car. "That's one of my business partners. You're gonna blow him off."

"What?"

"A blow job. Don't mess up my backseat though."

"I'm not giving him a blow job. What's wrong with you?" I nearly pushed Greene back but he caught my arm with a tight grip.

"I thought our arrangement was clear, you dumb bitch. Do what I say and you get what you want." He squeezed tighter.

"It's between me and you, not you and your-friends." I winched in pain from his grip.

"It's whatever I say it is so get your ass in that back seat and suck his dick or I'll make sure that you never get a hold of what you want." He threatened with a final squeeze of my arm.

My throat was tight and my vision slowly blurred as my emotions were in high. Greene stared me down and a smile slowly appeared on his face.

"Good girl. Now make it quick because I'm next." He released me and walked in the opposite direction of his car to leave me to service the unknown business man in his backseat.   • • •

• • •

The memory was an unflattering one considering that I currently held the very file that Greene had hovered over my head that very night. I'd done horrid things to try and obtain it but Donovan had handed it over without degrading me. He could've asked me to do anything and I probably would've done it.

But he knew I was a fool for trusting him. He knew before I even knew which was the absolute worst part because now I was on my way to the city with no way of redeeming my stupidity. I wasn't sure when I would ever see him again but I knew it would be incredibly different. Greene held me captive by contract but Donovan held me captive through his presence.

I hated not knowing what Donovan's intentions were and why I was in this position. But I also questioned why I even wanted answers since he was the first person in my life who had been consistent and who had given without taking.

I couldn't believe that I was allowing myself to hold him on a pedestal as if he weren't a criminal. It was crazy but for some reason I'd felt safe when I was with him and that was what I had wanted for so long.

"We were told not to stop for any reason so try and hold it for the next couple of hours." The guard next to me said.

"What?"

"Your leg is shaking. Figured you had to use the bathroom." He pointed to my leg. I hadn't noticed that reaction to thinking about Donovan.

"Oh no, I'm fine."

"Good, can't take any chances." He leaned forward near the driver. "You know I was just reading about Ashton in the paper. He was shaking hands with Senator Bradley."

"What did the boss say?" The driver asked. I was curious as well.

"When I mentioned it he said he wasn't surprised. Something about seeing Ashton's men at a restaurant. Maybe the senator tipped them off."

"The guys at the retaurant said Grace tipped them off." I interjected out of shear confusion. If we were in an area that a senator lived in and that very senator was shifting loyalty then that seemed like more of an issue with anyone being at the lake house.

The man sitting beside me looked at me and squinted. "Oh yeah? And who do you think Grace's father is?" He laughed, leaning back in the seat.

I appeared to be the only one shocked by this news. Donovan had been sleeping with Grace knowing that she was a prominent senators daughter? It all made sense now. This was why I was being forced away from Donovan. Ashton knew the best way to get information was through the senator who clearly wanted his daughter kept safe.

So she told her father about Donovan and the father told Ashton. How could they stay at the lake house with that risk?

"It's all a business." The man next to me said, as if reading my mind.

Before I could respond however, an impact was felt on the side of the car and it jolted both of us forward.

"Shit, what-" another harder impact was made to the car which caused the driver to swerve the wheel which made the car to skid out of control.

The guard next to me clumsily withdrew a gun from inside his breast pocket but by the time it was produced, I looked past him out the window and noticed a black van barreling toward us.

I screamed and shut my eyes as I felt the car we were in turn and flip on its side. It all happened so quickly and there was no time to process what had occurred as my body weakened and gave out sending me into a state of blankness. My eyes went from seeing a set of upside down black oxfords past the shattered glass window, to complete and utter darkness.   • • • • • •My body felt like it was tangled in barbwire and my head carried the weight of a brick. Nothing felt aligned even as I slowly felt myself regain consciousness and my eyes slowly adjusted to the sight before me.

I knew that the Range Rover had been smashed into by another van and that I'd been removed from the upturned vehicle a moment after. However, the rest of the events were a blur.

I gazed down and noticed that my left wrist was restrained by a chained cuff. Was I in jail again? This didn't look like a jail. Though the light was dim and brick walls surrounded me, there was a thick glass door that stood across the room giving a view of a row of luxury cars in the distance. As if it were part of a garage.

I tried to move and get a better view but as the chained tugged, pain soared through my body. Bruises and scratches were inevitably the cause of the pain. Even my mouth tasted of metallic and I was sure that my face was marked in even worse ways than I would be familiar with.

Where was Donovan? I needed him to help me make sense of this or I would descend into madness. Which I couldn't be far from since the past couple of weeks had been absolute torture for me. So whoever had brought me here was part of the crowd that could care less about my well-being.

"Ms. Rosemary." An unfamiliar voice called outside of the glass door. As much as I wanted answers I didn't want to meet someone new. Not in this current embarrassing state.

A tall figure appeared in my line of sight with a set of keys that unlocked the glass door. He sighed and flicked a switch that brought more light into the room. "Good, you're awake."

The brighter status of the room gave me a better view of what was inside and who the bald man was in front of me.

"You're pretty bruised up." He said, scanning me with his dark eyes. I knew that this meant trouble. It didn't matter who he was or where I was. All I knew was that I needed to stay as quiet as possible because I'd constantly gotten myself in trouble by speaking when I was with Donovan.

The bald man looked as if he were waiting for me to question him but when a minute went by and he didn't get what he expected, he spoke to again.

"I'm William Ashton." My eyes expanded at the name. I'd grown accustom to it in a negative context.

Ashton seemed pleased this time by my reaction because he chuckled and stepped closer. "Yes, in the flesh. But don't worry, I won't hold you accountable for what Donovan has said about me." He shook his head. "That wouldn't be fair. But I will be keeping you here with me for a while to draw him in. You're the bait."

I almost wanted to laugh at that. The joke was on him because Donovan didn't care about me enough to be lured in by Rosemary bait. He didn't even care that I'd been kidnapped en route to New York if he already knew about this. It was like dangling a piece of lettuce in front of a lion. Pointless.

"You're not usually this quiet." He said as if he'd known me all my life.

"How would you know?" I asked my first question.

"Let's just say-I knew people that knew you." He smiled and shrugged. I knew very few people as a whole so I didn't know who he could be referring to. "But since I won't be getting much from you, I'll just explain to you that I intend to keep you down here so unfortunately you don't have a bed but we'll feed you. When Donovan comes to 'save' you we'll kill him and then you're free to go. How does that sound?"

I pressed my lips together but immediately regretted it due to the pain. I didn't care anymore and I was sure it didn't matter how anything sounded to me. If Ashton really wanted to lure Donovan he would've kidnapped Hannah or Pharrah. But there was no point in me saying this aloud. They both had a lot more going for them and I wouldn't want either to be in my position.

I shut my eyes and rested my head back on the wall, refusing to open them even when I heard Ashton's footsteps leave the room. For the first time I felt defeated and exhausted by my condition. Mainly because I knew Ashton was lying. Whether he got Donovan or not, I was a dead woman walking either way.

Chapter Twenty Three: A Coincidence

"Alright, get up." A large man that had been sliding me food for the past two nights announced, fussing around with a few keys on a chain.

I backed closer to the wall, alarmed at his loud voice.

"What're you doing?" I asked, watching him approach me and pinch one of the smaller keys.

"Ashton wants to see you." I'd been almost three days of me being chained in this garage with simple portions of carb heavy foods that I barely touched.

Now Ashton wanted to see me? It had to be something bad.

The big man helped me to my feet and automatically the floor felt uneven as if it were rotating. I grabbed the wall to steady myself and waited to regain balance. My ass throbbed, my head pounded, and my mouth was dry. I needed a shower, a massage, and a bed but that was all too much to ask for.

Even as we approached the hallway my eyes were unfamiliar to the light. However, clarity came quick when Ashton appeared outside of an empty room that overlooked a large pool.

I hadn't been exposed to much sun or natural light in quite some time so it was refreshing to be able to see through long windows. Until Ashton pulled me to him and I heard the snip of scissors near my head. I backed away quickly, giving him a shove and then touching all around my head.

A chunk of hair was in between three of Ashton's fingers."Perfect. Derek, put this in an envelope and send it to Faust." He handed it over then smiled at me.

"How have you been Rosemary?"

"Not well." Clearly.

"Good." He seemed to not even hear my response. "I think you'll be interested to know that Donovan hasn't contacted me yet. So it seems you're not as valuable as I thought." Ashton shook his head and sighed. He was crazy.

"Then why did you cut my hair?" Ashton widened his eyes.

"Well, it's a last resort. I would've done the traditional finger but-" He pointed to his suit, "I would hate to get this bloody." I almost gagged at the thought of what this man was capable of. He was just like Greene.

"I want you to have dinner with me tonight. Then I want you to stay with me tonight."

"What?"

"Let's do dinner first. Then we'll discuss the rest. My assistant will take you to shower and get dressed." I didn't know what I was hearing but I knew that I was in the presence of a creep. Was he going to rape me? It was like a movie that I wanted no parts in.

I channeled the captive that had been with Donovan only a week prior to this moment and made another rash decision. Without a second thought, I pushed Derek aside and ran across the room, aiming for one of the tall windows.

"Rosemary, don't do this." He laughed as I tried to unlock the window. I didn't know what I was thinking but I wanted to leave and this was the only way I knew how to try and get out of any situation. "You shouldn't try and run, eventhough I know it's something you love to do." He said and I paused my failing mission to peak over my shoulder.

"How-" I gulped, turning around. "Why did you say that?"

Ashton put his hands in his pocket and took a step across the room."Oh, I haven't told you? When we collided with the car you were in, we found a file. I'm sure Greene would've wanted me to have it if we're being honest."

I almost broke down right then and there. He had my file but had he known Greene? It would explain so much if they were once acaquainted.

"Why did you say his name?"

"You seem confused. How about I explain it over the dinner you attempted to run from." He checked his watch and nodded. I nodded back, hoping to get an answer or two despite my feeling of discouragement. What could I do? I had no choices anymore, I was better off dead. • • • • • •I didn't touch the food in front of me. It looked delicious but my appetite was ruined and I wanted my file back from the monster. He knew he had information that I wanted so he slowly ate and awkwardly smiled at me every so often.

I was convinced that he was attracted to what he had made me wear to dinner. Black was morbid and if he killed me I would be dressed for a funeral. My red lips were the color of blood which added to the violent intention behind my evening attire. It terrified me more that his creepy eyes would constantly study me as he chewed on steak.

Donovan had to be the unicorn of organized crime because he was extremely handsome and charming to those he liked. Ashton was just unappealing to look at and awkward to watch. This could've been the reason why he despised Donovan so much.

"Greene was an associate of mine. Well, technically he was first an associate of Donovan's until I offered more money for him to work for me."

"Work how?"

"He supplied vacant spaces for us to conduct the more gruesome parts of business. Places that the police wouldn't find since the areas were desolate." Ashton took a sip of wine. "Greene mentioned you several times. So when he was murdered I knew who to start with. Your friend Charlotte was a big help." Our eyes met.

"Charlotte?!"

"Yes, that beautiful whore. Everyone has a price Rosemary. She wants to leave Lush so we made an-arrangement."

"What was the arrangement?" If I kept him talking then I would prolong the possibility of accompanying him to his room. Also, I wanted to be sure of why I was in this situation and if it meant hearing the worse things about my own friend then I had to be prepared.

"Ten thousand for any information you'd given her. She told Faust's men first but I convinced her to take my money." Ashton set his fork and knife down. "My issues with Donovan run deep but murdering Greene was the tipping point. Someone needed to show that man that he can't just play by his own rules and always lash out when things or people aren't in his favor. Wherever he tries to run-I'll find him." There was a demonic glint to his eyes that scared me because it made me realize how dangerous he could possibly be.

"Then you should've taken someone more important." I meant it. He chose the wrong hostage to teach Donovan a lesson with. I was worthless.

"Perhaps." He stared at me for what seemed like the longest few seconds of my life. "But Hannah's next anyway." I shot my head up.

"Hannah?" That was a death wish. If there was no sense of urgency with me then Ashton was in for a rude awakening.

"Yes, now that I know he's not coming for you Hannah's the next option." He stood up from his seat. "So here's what's going to happen; I'll keep you here for my personal needs, get Hannah, then kill you." He shrugged.

I bit down on my bottom lip and stared at him. There was nothing I could do. It was only a matter of when. When would he kill me.

The hardest part of all this was that I would never even get a chance to thank Hannah or Donovan for all they had done for me even if it wasn't much.

I stood up as well, but before I could ask to be excused to the bathroom, an alarm sounded in the room. The alarm wasn't very loud but it caused Ashton to twist his face in confusion.

"What is that?" I asked.

Ashton hurried to the window and peaked out the blinds. He didn't bother answering my question, he just grabbed my arm and pulled me out of the dining room and down the hall with haste.

No one was around, which was unlike the first house Donovan had kept me in where every so often a worker would pass. I didn't know what a empty house meant but I couldn't ask since I was being tugged harshly through spotless teal hallways with hard wood floors.

"Farrenger!" Ashton said when we finally spotted someone ahead.

Farrenger was rushing in our direction with a gun drawn. His name sounded awfully familiar.

"Bring her to the guest house sir. We have a disturbance in the courtyard."

"What type of disturbance?" Ashton seemed calm but I knew he was on edge.

"We don't know yet but it's best that you take her to the guest house. I'll call you when we find out." Farrenger looked past us the entire time he spoke then hurried forward before Ashton could respond. He exhaled loudly then looked down at me.

"If you had anything to do with this then I swear I'll kill you before you can even make it out of this place." He pulled my arm again through the hall and then down a flight of stairs that led to a hidden door.

We emerged into the darkness of a large yard that was illuminated by several soft garden lights. The large blue pool was also lit and aided in our journey to a small detached house nearby.

"We have to stay in there?" I asked, scared to be in a secluded place with him again. It was hard enough being at a dinner table just a moment ago.

"Yes," he stopped us outside the door, "unless you have an alternate option." He said sarcastically while pushing open the door. He pushed me forward into the house before following behind and shutting the door.

The house smelled of basement linens as if it hadn't been inhabited by anyone in months. But that would make sense because Ashton wasn't very pleasant so I didn't know who would want to stay with him in any capacity. I barely wanted to stand near him.

"Come on." He demanded, taking my arm again into the first room to our left. "Turn on the light switch." He said to me as if I knew the layout of his guest house. It was pitch black but I slid my hands along the wall nearest to me and flicked the first switch that I could find.

A golden light was cast into the living room where four other figures appeared in the space. I gasped at the sight and felt my body tense up. Ashton's grip on my arm tightened.

"Ashton," Donovan was seated on the arm of the chair but stood when he spoke. "A coincidence?"

Ashton's face was washed white in surprise and his Adam's apple bobbed as he swallowed a bundle of nerves. He shook his head.

"I wouldn't call it that." He replied, glancing frantically around the room at the foreign people. Nate was by the fireplace with his holster revealed, Lance sat by the window, and Phil was closest to Ashton and I by the doorway.

"Well I'm glad I found you." Donovan put his hands in his pockets and stepped to the center of the room. The closer he got, the safer I felt and the more hopeful I got. "Especially because I heard you were looking for me."

"I was. But not just you." Ashton said with a smirk. "Where's that angel Hannah?" He teased and Nate instinctively stepped forward with a hand on his gun but Donovan held a finger up to him.

Ashton reacted to Nate's threatening motion and pulled me to him, flicking out a seven inch blade that he placed right at my neck. "Don't do anything stupid or she's dead." Despite his shaky hand, he sounded relatively calm. Maybe it was because he had the power in that moment.

My heart rate increased and I tried to control my breathing because any movement could lead to a sliced throat.

Lance stood up slowly and looked at Donovan who kept his stance in the center of the room while his eyes met mine.

"Are you okay Rosemary?" He asked in a settled tone. Terrified, I didn't nod or move my head at all. I was okay for now and that was all he wanted to know.

"Yes." I said. Donovan gave a short nod and for a moment I thought he had given up to Ashton since I was in such a vulnerable position. However, what happened next defied the concept of time and probably physics because within a three second count, Donovan withdrew a hand gun from his holster and shot downward. My eyes quickly shut tight in order to bear the pain that would surge through my neck from the blade. But instead, the gunshot rang through my ears as I heard a loud shriek and felt the pressure of Ashton's body detach from me as he slumped to the ground.

In an instant Phil grabbed me to him and I watched as Donovan slowly approached Ashton's limp body, handing his gun to Lance.

Ashton cradled his bloody foot as crimson red blood stained the beige carpet. Donovan kicked aside the switch blade with his brown wing tips and looked down pitifully at Ashton. He squatted and placed a phone beside the bleeding body. Though my ears rang from the shot I could heard Donovan's distant voice.

"Tell Farrenger to clear the front so we can leave here with no further issues." Ashton grimaced louder from the pain. Donovan stood up. "Also, Tuesday morning we're meeting at The Ritz to discuss business. Just us." Though Ashton didn't respond due to the pain that he was probably in, we all knew that he wouldn't refuse.

Donovan approached me, ignoring the loud sounds of a grown man moaning in pain that circulated throughout the room.

"Can you walk?" I was quivering from the shock and my palms covered my ear, so I shook my head knowing that if Phil hadn't been holding me, I would've fallen over.

Donovan scooped me up bridal style and led the way out of the guest house with Nate, Lance, and Phil behind us. I wrapped my arms around his neck.

Once I was exposed to the outdoors I felt my head become light. It was either the shock or the chance of survival that caused me to pass out in Donovan's arms before we even reached the car.

Chapter Twenty Four: Back Home

I woke up in a bed that wasn't my own which wasn't much of a surprise since I hadn't been in my own bed for the past two or three weeks.

However, this bed in particular felt even more amazing than the one I'd melted in at the lake house. The bed sheets were a light charcoal color that enveloped my entire body and the thick pillows surrounded my head.

I pushed up and squinted due to the natural light that pierced through the large windows and flooded the room. I was in someone's bedroom, on someone's king sized bed, with someone's large shirt covering my bra set.

There wasn't much personalized furniture within the slate gray walls of the room, but it helped to know that I wasn't stuffed into a basement.

A knock sounded on the door across the room and before I could respond it swung open and Hannah appeared. I felt the tense grip that I had on the sheets soften instantly and I was completely reassured of my safety.

She grinned when she noticed that I was alert, set the wooden tray that she'd been holding on the edge of the bed, then rushed to give me a tight hug.

"I'm so happy to see you!" She gushed.

"Really?"

"Yes, of course!" She released me. "I hated that Ashton found out we were in separate cars." Hannah handed me a banana and a bottle of water. "But not as much as Donovan hated himself for everything I assume."

"Should I eat?"

"Yeah, have a couple bites before I give you this pain killer. There's more food downstairs." She explained.

"Where am I?" I asked as Hannah crossed the room to open the blinds wider on each window.

"Donovan's room. We figured no one would disturb you in here."

I peered out the window and saw the cloudy sky tucked behind staggered buildings and roof tops. "We're in the city?"

"Yeah," Hannah smiled, "we're back home." She placed her hands on her hips.

Home? Now even I knew that was a lie because it was a foreign word to me. She had even said "we" as if I belonged in this picture. Any other time I would've rolled my eyes but Hannah seemed to believe those words so I just stared at her blankly.

"And before you ask, please don't worry about Lush right now. I just really want you to rest up. There's no more hiding and no more hostage situations. I promise." Hannah reassured though, again, I wasn't quite sure if I believed her. I trusted, her but I didn't know if I could believe her for this.

I moved to the side of the bed and grabbed the banana, taking a small bite.

"There're some clothes on that chair for you and and there's a towel in the bathroom as well." She pointed to the chair by the window and then to the doorway leading to the bathroom. "Come downstaires when you're ready to eat. If you're not feeling up to it then I'll bring food up here to you." I nodded and waited until Hannah left to head into the bathroom.

For the first time I felt as if I were more safe than usual. I'd taken an actual hot shower without fear of wasting the hot water supply or being rushed to finish. I was wearing clothes that were straight off the racks and still had tags on them. Maybe a white blouse and pants weren't seen as luxury items to some but they'd clearly cost a pretty penny and Hannah had gone out her way to buy gold jewelry as well for me.

It was all so new to me after everything I'd been through. Even walking through the penthouse apartment to the kitchen was a different feeling to me because I was free to know my current situation as opposed to all the other times when I was oblivious.

Hannah and Pharrah were being the island of the kitchen when I walked in. Pharrah was hovering over a waffle maker and Hannah was pouring a glass of cranberry juice.

"Have a seat Rosemary, Pharrah made waffles." She gave me the cranberry juice while Pharrah came to slide a few waffles onto my plate. Her expression was different than I remembered. She was a lot less enthusiastic. Maybe Donovan hadn't proposed yet.

"Thank you." I looked down at the food pleasantly surprised.

"Good morning." I heard a new voice enter the kitchen. Glancing over my shoulder provided a pleasant surprise as Donovan approached in a deep green shirt that gave him a warmer exterior than I was use to. My heart sped up with boarderline excitement from the sight of him, the same reaction I'd had last night when he rescued me.

"Good morning. Ashton called asking for you earlier this morning. Also, on an unrelated note, would you like coffee or tea?" Hannah leaned on the counter.

Donovan touched the back of my chair. "Coffee please." His back went to the two other women so that he could face me after responding. "How're you feeling?" He asked. He didn't look as if he'd been up all night even though I knew the drive from Ashton's had been a long one.

"I'm okay." I tried to avoid studying him too hard since I knew my mind would run wild from how close we were.

"The doctor's going to come see you today. Hannah will let me know how it goes."

"Where'll you be?" I asked as Hannah set a cup of coffee down for Donovan.

"I'll be here tonight." He answered reassuringly as if he knew I would feel more secure with him present.

"Donovan, stop distracting Rose from eating." Hannah insisted, staring down at her phone while leaning sideways on the counter.

Donovan chuckled and took a single sip of coffee then set it aside. "Call Ashton back and put all of Rosemary's stuff in my room." He told Hannah before grabbing an apple from the fruit bowl and heading out of the kitchen.

Pharrah was gone when I turned back from watching Donovan leave. Hannah followed my gaze at the empty waffle maker and smiled mischeviously.

"Today's her last day working for Donovan."

"Why?"

"Because you're all he's been talking about."

"I was kidnapped." I cocked an eyebrow assuming that common sense and sympathy were lacking in this equation.

"She's an idiot." Hannah shrugged. "Eat up. We have to see the doctor and get the rest of your clothes from the store."

I didn't want to see the shady doctor but if Donovan requested it then I had to go. What I wanted most however, was answers about everything that happened last night because I still wasn't sure about one thing: did Donovan actually care about me?

Chapter Twenty Five: Cause of Death

Donovans apartment was the size of a luxury hotel but had some of the personality and charm of a Brooklyn studio. Hannah had informed me that the Upper East Side penthouse was the permanent residence of the Boss. It was also the permanent residence of Stone, who had an embroidered doggy bed that he laid on by the fireplace in the living room.

"This is the library. Believe it or not Donovan handpicked all the books in here with some help from his father." I looked at the built in shelves that covered all four walls. It was hard to believe that Donovan took time out of his schedule to pick out books when he hardly had time to eat breakfast in the morning.

"It's beautiful." I probably said for the tenth time that day.

"Isn't it. Aside from the business, it's the only thing his father passed on to him so he appreciates it a lot." She placed her hands on her hips. "Donovan has a sensitive-" her ringtone sounded before she could finish her statement. "Hello...no I can't do that without his permission...he's not even here..." Hannah held up her finger to me and then walked out of the library.

I didn't wait for her to return. I was getting anxious to see and talk to Donovan. There was also an unsettling feeling in my stomach that the large apartment made me vulnerable. Ashton could be anywhere. So I found my way back to Donovan's room and shut the door so that I could be in a smaller, more secure place.

I went into his walk-in closet which had rows of tailored suits, racks of designer ties, Italian leather shoes, and multiple watches behind a frosted glass case.

I grabbed a throw blanket from the room, returned to the closet, and shut my eyes, sinking into the plush rug that covered the space.

• • • • • •My eyes only shot open when I heard the loud shutting of a door and through the open closet doorway I watched as Donovan sauntered into the room. He stopped just before the bed while stripping off his green shirt, then turned to see me cuddled in his closet.

"Comfortable?" He asked. I was a bit embarrassed by how I probably looked.

"I was scared." I admitted. He walked over to me with a low sigh.

"He's never going to be near you again." Donovan said but I wondered how he could be sure of that? "Did the check up with Thornton go well?"

"He said I'm okay but he wants to see me again if the bruises don't fully heal in a couple days."

"Bruises?" I nodded, showing Donovan my legs and pulling my shirt collar to the side so he could see my torso. The car accident and cuffs had taken a toll on my body even days later. There were several scratches on me as well but the doctor had been hopeful that those would heal in due time.

Donovan crouched down beside me to get a closer look. Then his eyes met mine with a tenderness that I was unfamiliar with.

"I'm sorry." He said in a tone barely above a whisper. I held his gaze like a lost puppy because I didn't know why he was apologizing. Donovan Faust didn't apologize. That was a proven fact. And no one expected him to apologize, especially not to me.

"You didn't do it." I shrugged.

Donovan stood up and held out a hand to help me to my feet.

"Sleep in my bed tonight. I'll be in the room next door if you need me."

"I'm not tired anymore. I wouldn't be able to make myself fall back asleep anyway." Plus, Donovan was here which meant I could finally get some answers. I hadn't thought about the events of last night that much because I was scared of the memories. But I had so much to ask Donovan.

"Well in that case," he pointed to the bed, "I have something for you but I need you to sit down." He insisted. I obeyed and sat at the edge of the bed while he opened his side table drawer and pulled out what I'd been hoping to see for ages.

"Where-where did you find it?"

"We raided Ashton's study." He held the folder out to me. "It's finally yours again." I nodded, feeling my throat tighten as I grabbed it. Holding it again was reassuring and I knew this was the time to open it because I never wanted to be in a position where my information was held captive. Donovan must've sensed this because he motioned to leave the room.

"No, wait." I stopped him. "Can you stay please?" I asked. Donovan didn't respond but he returned to me and stood beside me at the foot of the bed.

I took a deep breath before reaching into the folder and pulling out the loose sheets that contained my life story. I didn't scan it thoroughly because the typed content was overwhelming. However, I did notice the handwritten details that were in traditional cursive.

Name: Rosemary HurstBirthdate: May 2,...Parent(s)/Guardian(s): Gregory Hurst & Daisy HurstStatus: DeceasedCause of Death: Car Collision

My body went numb at the last line and my vision slowly clouded as I looked up at Donovan. He took the file from my tightened grip then grabbed a Kleenex from his bedside table.

I felt myself getting weak and breathing heavily from the information I'd just read. I burrowed my face in the bed as the tears emerged uncontrollably from my eyes. I cried because I'd never felt a full identity being in the foster stystem. I cried because they'd always told us that we were born on the same day so that we wouldn't question anything. I cried because my parents had existed at one point. I cried because I was just finding this out after years of anxiety and misery.

"I have to leave." I said in a muffled tone since my face was still buried.

"Where?" Donovan asked. I slowly turned to look at him because he had asked a great question. Where would I go? I had nothing and tonight solidified that.

"I-I don't know Donovan. I feel-I feel-lost..." • • • • • "Are you lost?" Greene asked behind me.

I cursed under my breath since he'd found me like this. Rummaging through his belongings in only my lace bra and panties, kneeling in front of his desk draw. I nervously chuckled and looked over my shoulder.

"No, I was looking for something." I pushed off of the ground and stood. "I thought you were asleep."

"I was." He looked at the draw curiously. "Then I heard you making noise."

"Sorry, I didn't mean to wake you up." He narrowed his eyes.

"What're you looking for?"

"Uh, my earrings. I left them here last week so I figured I would look for them." I lied but it was better than admitting that I was looking for the folder that he clearly hid better than his Viagra pills.

"Are you lying to me?" He stared at me hard. I sighed and grabbed my dress from the sofa.

"No, Steven." He was about to be in a mood and I didn't want to deal with it.

"Yes you are. You were looking for that fucking file." He smirked with his hands on his hips like an arrogant asshole. I slid into the dress and grabbed my purse.

"Sure."

"And what were you going to do when you found it?" He chuckled. "Leave Lush? Leave New York?" Actually I hadn't thought past finding the damn thing. I knew I would never want to see Greene again but where would I go? I didn't have any family or at least I didn't think I did.

"Maybe you and I could travel the world." He mocked, laughing at my misery. I rolled my eyes.

"I'd die before traveling anywhere with you." I finally said, fed up with how he was taunting me. Greene stopped laughing and looked at me with a serious expression.

"Die?" He repeated, taking slow steps closer to me. "It's funny you say that." I didn't know why it was funny. I had been serious but apparently so was he.

"Funny?"

"Well, it's ironic. Maybe one day you'll realize that death is closer to you than you think."

"Are you threatening to kill me?" I asked quietly. He did scare me at times and I think he knew it.

Greene chuckled, reaching into his pocket and licking the tip of his finger to flip through a stack of bills.

"Not at all Cinnamon." He held two hundred dollar bills in front of my face. I took the money from his pinched fingers as he continued to speak. "Because if I really wanted to kill you, you'd be dead already."

Chapter Twenty Six: Shattered Pieces

I must've cried so much that eventually my body was drained of tears. So I laid on my side, staring out the window across the room as the darkened sky turned to a light indigo.

Donovan stepped out of the room for a while after I had stopped crying but twenty minutes later he returned with a bottle of cold water and a white washcloth.

"Hold this to your face." He wet the cloth with the water and held it out to me. I sat up and pressed it under my eyes for a few minutes. I probably looked like a tomato with my swollen face and flushed cheeks but I didn't care because there was so much more happening in my mind.

"C'mon Rosemary." Donovan opened the bedroom door and looked at me to follow him. I didn't feel the need to question him so I stood up slowly from my place and walked out of the room. Maybe he would take me out of my misery by putting me in another basement. That way I could be left alone to wallow in my thoughts.

Donovan came behind me and led me through the apartment and into a private elevator that brought us to the front of the building. The streets of New York were desolate and quiet at this time before the sunrise but the cool breeze was refreshing considering my current state of mental suffocation.

The doorman handed Donovan a set of keys and guided us toward a black Tesla parked in the front. Donovan opened the door for me then slid behind the wheel.

We drove for almost an hour out of the city and through suburban land in silence. I didn't want to speak, I just wanted to process my life. Not that Donovan expected me to say anything because for the first time since I'd met him, he was seeing a deeper side of my life that I'd essentially invited him into. It was hard not to though. Greene had known everything and continued to torture me because he knew I'd do anything to be released from his hold. Donovan on the other hand, hurt me in the beginning but was the one who returned my life back. It was difficult to understand.

Donovan stopped the car but I didn't get out of my daze until my passenger door opened and he helped me out. The sky had lightened gradually so I had a better view of the place around me. I stared up at Donovan in awe as he draped a jacket over my shoulders.

"They're this way." He nodded to the left and walked me away from the car until we stopped by two granite headstones.

I took a deep breath and looked down at them for who knows how long. Re reading the text on my parents headstone allowed their names to sink in and also the date of their passing: June 14, 1997. I needed this as a form of closure. It wasn't going to answer all of my questions but it was a start.

For them to have received a formal burial meant that someone had to plan it which meant I probably had family out there somewhere. But only time would tell and for right now I was content with this so that it wasn't too overwhelming.

I let out a heavy sigh and nodded, looking up at Donovan again who had stood in silence the entire time. A part of me wanted to ask him how he'd tracked down my parents in such a short period of time. But the other part of me knew the answer already. His business made things like this work by whatever means.

"I'm ready to leave." I finally said after we had possibly stood there for thirty minutes.

Donovan furrowed his brows and asked, "Are you sure?"

"Yeah, I'm sure." He asked no further questions as we walked back to the car.

It would take me a while to be at peace with the reality of my life and the shattered pieces it was in. But I was okay with being patient to figure that out and put the pieces together.

However, I wasn't okay with why Donovan seemed to care so much. He'd stayed with me and let me cry within the last few hours. Why? I was his captive, then his object to protect, and now what? All of a sudden he cared about my actual life outside of Lush and his crime syndicate. I didn't want to believe that he cared about me as an individual because once I got close to anyone they betrayed and hurt me. That was why I survived this situation, because I hadn't gotten close to anyone except Hannah and it was safer that way.

My gentle feelings quickly turned to frustration and anger as we drove away from the cemetery. I had to say something to Donovan before I reached my boiling point. Most importantly, now that I felt a bit of closure about my family, I had to say something to Donovan to get closure from him before he threw me aside like the rest of the men in my life had.

Chapter Twenty Seven: Louder Baby

S tone approached us both when we walked back into the penthouse. I was sure that I surprised Donovan by not running away but the truth was that I was exhausted and my mind was whirling. Donovan was surely on the same boat as me since he yawned into the pit of his arm as he set his car keys down on the foyer table.

Part of me wished that Hannah was here just so that I could have a reason to not confront Donovan. But I would see her in a few hours regardless and tell her about my parents, right before telling her that I no longer wanted to be here with Donovan because I didn't know if I trusted him. It was too good to be true and there were so many unanswered questions in my mind.

"Where's the guest room?" I asked, turning to face him in the hallway. Donovan shook his head and turned my body around to lead me to the familiar door at the end of the hall.

"Donovan, can you tell me-"

"I'd rather you sleep in here." He admitted, shrugging out of his jacket.

I watched his casual movements throughout the room and felt my body heat up. I couldn't hold in my anger anymore. It had been boiling from the very first day I'd met Donovan and I'd never been given the proper outlet to express it. I needed to say something to him now.

"Why're you doing this?" I sat on the bed in confusion.

"Doing what?" I delayed my response so that he could consider the answer to his own question but I slowly realized that he was pre occupied with something in the closet.

"Why did you find me Donovan?"

"We were alerted about the collision." He walked out and handed me a new pajama set. "Then we did what we needed to do on our end to locate Ashton's place." He was giving me the generic business response instead of the actual details.

"But why did you find me? Why did you even care?" I pressed on. Donovan wore his frustration on his face.

"Rosemary, we've been up since two. I'm not doing-"

"Why did you even care?! You didn't have to look for me so why did you?" I yelled at him for the first time and didn't regret it.

Donovan walked across the room to shut the bedroom door then came back over to me, holding my gaze for the longest second I'd ever experienced.

"Change and go to sleep."

"Don't change the subject. Answer my questions." I demanded. Donovan scoffed, taking off his shirt and showing me that refined build that I'd slept beside in the lake house.

"Ask me again." He walked slowly toward me. I stood up to meet his steps, putting my hands on my hips defiantly.

"Why do you care Donovan? Why-" before I could get the rest of my words out, he tugged my body to his with a pinch of my white blouse.

"No more." His raspy voice was low as he took my chin inbetween his fingers while his hand wrapped around my body.

"No more what?" I asked, distracted by his warm touch.

Donovan started to unbutton my blouse but kept his green eyes glued to mine. I felt my breath caught in my throat as my nerves began to respond to the intensity of the moment.

"No more talking." My bra was revealed before he took a hold of my ass. "Unless you're saying my name." He hoisted me off the ground and pressed his lips to mine hungrily. Donovan's lips were soft but were juxtaposed by the fervor in which he embraced me.

I hit at his shoulders but it was a weak attempt at pretending to resist. I knew that I wanted this so bad and my body betrayed me by writhing against him like a nymphette.

Donovans had gripped my ass tighter and I feared that he would feel the dampness if he moved only a couple inches lower. It was a quick reaction to what I expected to happen.

"Donovan." I moaned when our lips separated.

"Mmm just like that." He whispered into my ear as he set me down onto the satin bed sheets. I backed up on the bed but watched him as he watched me, wiping his bottom lip with his thumb.

"I thought this wasn't a good idea for us." I recollected his words from the night of our foreplay session while we were hiding at the lake house.

"It still isn't." He moved to hover over me. "But I need to fuck you Rosemary." Donovan weaved his fingers through my hair.

"I-I want-I do-I want you to fu-fuck me." I stuttered nervously as if I no longer knew how to form coherent sentences out of simple words. Donovan smirked then gave my hair a rough pull.

"Take off your clothes." I gasped at the feeling of being ordered by him and quickly complied, trying to strip myself as he kissed along my neck. But I obviously wasn't quick enough because Donovan got impatient and took to stripping my pants off with swift certainty. My pussy creamed at his touch and I jerked away from him for fear that I would lose control of my own body.

"Donovan I-I'm really-" I gulped and Donovan's eyes traveled downward from my breasts. He touched my thigh and spread it open just enough to see what I had planned to confess. I was dripping through the blue boyshorts and it thrilled Donovan so much that he pulled the fabric to the side to get a better view of my glistening sex. I inhaled deeply, leaning back on my elbows.

"You did that." I accused. Donovan chuckled then bent between my legs and gave my bud a kiss, basking in my reaction.

"I know." He looked up at me. "Be a good girl and tell me what you want."

"I want you inside me." I said the words so low that I was surprised he didn't tell me to repeat myself. Donovan propped himself up and began undoing his own pants.

"That's really what you want?" I nodded. Was he asking because I was expected to be intimidated by his dick? I'd seen enough in my life so what made-

"Shit!" I exclaimed when it emerged before me. I hadn't realized that I'd said it allowed and immediately I felt blood rush to my cheeks which became rosy from embarrassment. I'd always hated commenting on Lush clients' dicks because they were all an odd size and I didn't want to give false hope. But I was reminded of how perfect his was and it was something I'd gladly suck dry again, especially attached to such a beautiful man.

Donovan touched the back of my head and lowered my mouth onto his member before I took the matter into my own hands and began to work the shaft and the head in a slow circular motion. However, I should've known that he wouldn't accept the pace for long since half way through I began gagging and slobbering on him as he controlled my head movements.

He grunted at the sloppy display and then took a hand full of my hair to pull me off before he lost control.

He stood up off of the bed and brought me to my feet as I wiped my mouth. I wanted him inside of me more than anything and I wanted it now.

We backed into the arm chair by the window and he gestured for me to sit on his lap. I didn't hesitate to place my hands on his shoulders.

"When was your last time?" He asked, rubbing my clit as I straddled his lap.

"Last year." I confessed, biting my lip from the intense feeling that soared through my core.

"So you and Greene nev-"

"No, no, no, not at all. No." I said quickly. A year ago I'd found myself with one of Charlotte's friends but I never let Greene touch me that way. Aside from him not being allowed to but then again he broke whatever rules he wanted to.

A small smirk came across Donovan's lips and he lifted me so that my legs were comfortably on either side of him. A year had been so long ago and lowering myself onto him proved to be a challenge that required deep breaths despite the natural lubrication. His size was intimidating and when he threw his head back I knew that my tight entrance was just as intimidating. But after several strokes of his incredible dick, my body responded hungrily and his hands gripped my hips as I bounced in place with him.

It was the most incredible sexual feeling and only got better as he pulled me to him and took tender licks at my nipples while keeping a tight grip on my hips and ass.

"Donovan-it's-so-good."

"Say it louder baby."

"Fuck me!" I clawed at his back as he brought his hand to my throat and squeezed. "Oh my god!" I was going over the edge.

Donovan choked me a bit harder as I bounced up and down. I couldn't hold back any longer and after a few last strokes I released with a low moan. He wasn't too far behind and moments later, I felt the warm feeling on my back.

I fell forward, panting as my head rested on his chest and we both descended from an orgasmic high. I knew that if I tried to move I would collapse from the lack of energy my body had left.

Donovan pushed forward to stand up and carried me to the bed. I bit my lip and sighed, slowly rolling over to my stomach in order to reach the Kleenex box on the opposite side. But just as my back was to him I heard Donovan exhale deeply and felt him wrap his arms around my body again.

"Don't tease me." He whispered into my ear. I moaned at those words and gripped the sheets as I felt him enter me again slowly from behind.

"It's too big." I bit down hard but didn't hesitate to meet his slow strokes as we entered round two. Donovan chuckled in my ear.

"And you're too tight." He placed his hands on my thighs and pushed. "So open up for me baby." I almost came at the soothing tone of his voice in contrast to his aggressive demands but kept it together because I didn't want this experience to end.

He was slowly stroking into me in, a different energy from our first round. But the slow strokes didn't come without ear biting and strong hands gripping my wrists to pin them behind me. The position only allowed for him to maintain full control so he took advantage by speeding up his pace.

"Shit, Do-Donovan-I-I can't-" I tried to form a sentence but my fast breaths prevented it.

"Not yet." He warned, slapping my ass. I tried to twist but he kept me grounded in pure ecstasy.

"Please-oh my god-" I knew he was getting off on preventing me from cumming and I wondered if this had been what I was missing all my life. The control. The tender passion through rough sex. The power. I loved it from Donovan and I didn't know if I could go on without it.

"Please Donovan!"

"Cum Rose." He allowed and I released all over his member while he followed suit seconds later.

Donovan rolled off of me as we both let our heavy breathing fill the silence of the room. Donovan sat up shortly after and pulled me further into the bed so that my head was physically on the pillow. I turned to say something but by then he was making his way into the bathroom.

My body was too tired to follow so I let my eyes flutter close so that I could gather all the energy that Donovan had drained from me.

Chapter Twenty Eight: Perfect Pawn

For the first time since I'd been in Donovan's possession, I woke up with him next to me.

The natural light illuminated his blonde hair and the sun kissed glow of his skin, which further confirmed his perfection. Perfect hair, perfect body, perfect fuck...

Wait, fuck. Donovan and I had had sex earlier this morning. Twice! And I could feel the tenderness between my legs from the impact of his size. It had been more than just amazing sex. Maybe it had been the passion I'd been missing for all of these years. But would he even remember? To him, I was probably another notch that meant nothing. So I wouldn't mention it. I couldn't mention it.

I slid out of the bed slowly, trying not to wake Donovan as I made my way to the bathroom. A hot shower would bring me to reality.

After getting dressed, I went downstairs, following the smell of cinnamon oatmeal and roasted coffee.

Hannah was at the breakfast bar, sipping from a mug while an unfamiliar man whistled with a pan and spatula in hand.

"Good morning." I said. Hannah and the man looked up.

"You look-radiant." She narrowed her eyes. I shrugged, grabbing a mug. "This is Dave, he's the new chef." I smiled at him while he set a bowl of oatmeal in front of me. "I decided to go the male route after Pharrah left. Now Donovan can stop giving women false hope." She only partly joked. It made complete sense especially for a man who claimed to not mix business with personal.

"What should I do today?" I asked because I didn't know how long I was supposed to stay here and mooch off of Donovan.

Hannah cocked her head in thought. "Well, Donovan has a meeting with Ashton in a couple hours so we have to work around that. But once that meeting is done we'll all have some answers." She checked the time on her phone then looked back at me.

"Where's your apartment with that lady Charlotte?"

"It's in the Village." I hadn't been there in so long. "Where's yours?"

"A few buildings down from this one." She looked past me and smiled. "There he is."

Donovan was fastening the cuff links of his dark blue suit as he approached. He paused when he saw the chef then gave Hannah a nod of approval.

"Your meeting is at 1:00 at The Ritz."

"Rosemary," he said. I cursed under my breath but looked up at him. "I know it's not ideal but you'll have to be in the car while the meeting takes place. Hannah and Lance will be with you."

I felt a bit anxious knowing that I might see Ashton again but I whole heartedly trusted Donovan now. So I nodded "yes". • • • • • •That afternoon, Phil drove Donovan to The Ritz in one car while Lance drove Hannah and I in another, parking across the street.

After about fifteen minutes, Nate appeared, sliding into the passengers seat and not bothering to great anyone else in the car before speaking to Lance.

"They found Grace. Ashton was keeping her at his place upstate."

"Well Donovan will be pleased to hear that."

"She wants nothing to do with us apparently." Nate shrugged.

"I don't blame her. She knew the rat, he probably threw her under the bus first." Lance laughed.

I drew my eyes away form the window and looked at Nate.

"Speaking of the rat." Nate patted his breast pocket. "We already have the warehouse set up for all three of-"

Hannah cleared her throat loudly, causing Nate to jump at the sudden sound. "Shouldn't you be talking about this in a different setting?" She asked rhetorically. Nate turned to look between the two of us.

"Lance why didn't you say anything?"

"I thought you saw them."

"No." Nate sighed in frustration. "I'm sorry, I didn't realize Donovan added the two of you to this trip."

"What trip?" I asked. Hannah shook her head.

"We found out a lot in the past few days and Donovan wants to fill you in." So I would finally get some answers after all this time.

"Why is he meeting with Ashton alone?" I asked. I heard a click sound and noticed Lance putting a clip into a gun.

"Because that's the way we do business. Very-organized." Lance smiled and Nate chuckled lightly. His words left a sour taste in my mouth and I was relieved an hour later when Donovan came out of The Ritz with Ashton wielding a thick mahogany cane as he limped to keep up. The two men said a few final words to each other then parted ways.

Lance and Nate got out of the car to talk to Donovan while I chose the very moment to practice my skill of reading lips. I was unsuccessful but either way I didn't need to try for long because when the back door opened, Donovan motioned for me to follow him.

"Everything you own is in Charlotte's apartment?" He asked.

"Yes." I didn't own much.

Donovan looked at Nate who gave him a confirmation nod before getting back into the car. Then we walked over to the familiar black Tesla where Phil stood, straightening up when he saw us approach.

"Make sure you drop Hannah off first." Donovan said, taking the Tesla key from Phil. "Then head out with Nate and Lance but be careful."

"Of course Boss." Phil nodded his head then walked away from us as we got into the black car.

"What's happening?" I asked. Donovan didn't bother to respond. He revved up the car and sped away which frustrated me even more than him not responding. I was tired of being kept in the dark even if it was for my safety. Silence had gotten me nothing but a custom cell in Aston's mansion and a plethora of bruises on my body.

"Donovan stop!" I screamed and to my surprise, Donovan stopped the car abruptly on an open road. How long had we been driving? I didn't recognize where we were but I knew it was outside of the city so it must've been thirty minutes. "Tell me something. Anything. Please." I met his eyes and could see that he was conflicted with something.

Donovan sighed, "when were you going to tell me about Charlotte selling you out?"

I gulped then toyed with the sleeves of my shirt. I honestly had forgotten about Charlotte's involvement in my kidnapping and the Greene situation. Either that, or I buried it deep, knowing that if I said anything at all she would get hurt.

"I'm sorry."

"She should be sorry." He pointed to nothing in particular. "She got you in this mess."

I couldn't speak. There was nothing to say because he was absolutely right. Charlotte had said that she cared about me but the entire time she had been more concerned about monetary gain.

"When I got that note the night that we left for the lake house, Ashton said he had a witness to connect you to the murder of Greene. She was going to be the witness."

"She was going to lie?" I asked. Donovan studied my face then shook his head in disbelief.

"Don't be so gulliable Rose." He said. "You didn't keep your mouth shut with Charlotte and if the police got a hold of you, you wouldn't keep your mouth shut with them. So if you want to know the reason we hid you, that's why."

"You thought I would snitch? Like Charlotte?"

"Yes, and I stand by it. But," Donovan began with a more gentle tone, "I also realized that you could help with an alibi, not now obviously, but at the time you were the perfect pawn."

"You were using me Donovan?!"

"Don't act so surprised Rose." He scoffed. "And who the hell are you really mad at?" I considered his words. He was right, again, I had put Charlotte on such a pedestal for so long because of her positive presence in my life so I found it hard to blame her. However, she didn't care about me since she'd fed Ashton information while Donovan was hiding me which meant,...

"Wait, Anthony's the rat?" I gaped, recalling Nate's words in the car. Donovan started up the engine.

"Anthony told Charlotte the town we were hiding in and he told her about Grace." He shook his head. "All for some pussy."

"My head hurts from all of this." I leaned back in the seat, feeling weak and overwhelmed. If I had been wrong about trusting Charlotte than I could be wrong about anyone. Even Hannah, even Donovan. But something in me was hopeful and that was a feeling that was rare for me.

Donovan nodded his head, "I know." He assured. "But you're safe now." • • • • • •I was sitting on the porch that night when I finally felt as if a weight had been physically lifted from my shoulders. I felt lighter, not because there was a cool breeze flowing over my exposed skin and through my hair. But rather, because for the first time, I had answers in my life. My parents, my birth, the cause of my situation, my relationship with Charlotte. Being held by Donovan had helped me gain sight of who I really was. I didn't want to go backward. But how could I go forward from here?

"Here." Donovan came into my line of sight with a pear. "You haven't eaten since this morning." Had it been that long?

"Thank you." I smiled up at him and took the fruit. "You have a nice view on the terrace. If I lived here I would be outside all the time."

"If I had the time, I would be outside all the time too."

"Find someone else to run your business. Then you'll be able to." I nudged him playfully. Donovan leaned on the glass partition.

"It's never that simple." He folded his arms. "You know better than anyone how hard it is to get out of some things." I nodded slowly in response.

"Well, I'm sure from an organized crime standpoint, you're the best in the business." I said. Donovan chuckled lightly and went over to open the sliding glass door.

"I'm serious!" I said, looking over my shoulder. "You found out everything and still managed to keep me safe for some reason. You could've killed me."

Donovan shrugged, "Yeah, I could've." I stood from the chair to face him.

"Why didn't you?"

"Don't ask questions. Just consider yourself lucky." He smirked down at me.

"Is Ashton lucky too? Since you didn't kill him?" I couldn't stand the thought of murder anymore but Donovan made it so hard to understand his motives.

"Don't compare yourself to Ashton." He slid the door closed as I stepped into the warmth of the penthouse apartment. "Ashton will be-handled."

His words made my stomach turn so I reached to stop Donovan from walking further ahead of me.

"Can I ask you another question?" He nodded, a bit confused at my sudden impulse to halt him. "What's going to happen to Charlotte?" I knew it was a question that I shouldn't care to ask given what she'd done but I had to know.

Donovan pressed his lips together as he focused on my worried expression.

"She'll be dealt with." He said plainly. I fidgeted with my hands.

"Just please don't-don't kill her." I pleaded. Donovan narrowed his eyes.

"You know, she's the reason Ashton targeted you in the-"

"I know, I know." I sighed, "I know what she did but-she's helped me in the past even if it wasn't genuine and-and I know how it feels to want to get out of Lush. Especially now that-I've met you." I admitted, feeling a bit embarrassed for confessing too much.

Donovan followed my head as it sulked. He stepped closer to me.

"Look at me." He demanded. I quickly did so. "Charlotte will be dealt with the way I see fit."

"But please don't-"

"Did you hear me?" I looked into his eyes as best I could because I knew that what he meant to ask was if I trusted him. This was out of my control entirely but I hoped that whatever happened to Charlotte, it would all be okay in the end. Either way, Donovan didn't take demands or requests so I had to stop talking and just give a response.

"Yes Donovan." I finally said. Donovan was pleased with my response because the corner of his lips turned slightly upward as he took my hand into his.

He leaned down and kissed my cheek tenderly, as if I were a delicate rose petal.

"Are you staying with me tonight?" He asked in almost a whisper. I let out a barely audible "Yes" eventhough I knew that it was a bad choice because in less than twenty four hours I would no longer have the option to lay next to Donovan. I knew that the blissful beating of my heart as he lead me upstairs would come to an end. I knew that the gentle kiss on my cheek would fade shortly. All in twenty four hours.

But for now, I would relish in the short but meaningful time I had with Donovan.

CHAPTER TWENTY NINE: THANK YOU

I think I preferred overcast days as opposed to a sunny day like today. On a sunny day, we were expected to go out and have plans or else it was considered a waste of time. On an overcast day, the expectation didn't exist.

But my life had never really been planned to my satisfaction. So a sunny day to me wasn't exactly hopeful or eventful, it was confusing. Especially today since my mind wasn't in a hopeful state.

Hannah and Donovan were still upstairs but Nate and I continued to the entrance of the apartment building with my only suitcase in hand.

In the beginning, I'd had no possessions with me but after Hannah had gone on a shopping spree for me I was able to leave with something tangeable to keep. Everything else I would have to leave behind.

Although I didn't exactly know what was happening, I knew last night would be the last time that I would sleep in Donovan's apartment. But where would I go now?

"Is Donovan sending me back to Lush?" I finally asked.

"Lush is shut down as of tomorrow because of the trouble Charlotte caused." Nate said, shoving his hands into his pockets.

So what was I supposed to do? Where would I live? Where would I work? Charlotte had been "handled" so there was no way that her apartment was open for me anymore. She probably didn't even want to see me, if she happened to still be alive!

I felt my chest begin to tighten and I tried my best to control my breathing. It became harder to control as I noticed Donovan walk out of the building entrance and nod to the doorman.

He approached us in his more comfortable attire of a leather jacket and t-shirt as if today was just another mundane day for him. It probably was. But for me, it was anything but mundane.

He began to speak but stopped when he noticed my uneasy demeanor. "What's wrong?"

"Nothing, just waiting on the cars to-"

"I wasn't asking you." Donovan said to Nate. He turned back to me and studied my expression. "Nate, can you go and see if Hannah needs help."

Nate quickly caught the hint and turned on his heels to go back inside the building.

"Did something happen while I was-"

"I don't know what I'm supposed to do." I interrupted, feeling a minor anxiety episode happening. "Will Roth pay me?"

"This is about Lush." Donovan said and I nodded eventhough he hadn't asked a question.

A moment later, a black Mercedes Benz pulled up and Lance stepped out of the passengers seat.

"Hey Boss, we're ready to head out." Now I really felt the pressure. "Head out" where? They were all going to leave me. As my breaths quickened Donovan held up a finger and then took me aside to make our conversation more private.

"Where do you expect me to go?" I felt my voice raise because there was a possibility that I'd be thrown away again.

"Calm down." Donovan touched my arms gently. "Deep breaths." I complied as he rubbed my arms and waited for my breathing pace to return to normal. His touch was oddly soothing and even his calm expression helped center me. "There's nothing for you back at Charlotte's apartment or any other clubs that Roth owns."

I turned as I noticed Hannah and Nate exit the building together but Donovan didn't let my eyes wander too long as he stepped back into my line of sight.

"Rosemary."

"Yes?" I felt defeated. Again. As if I'd been trapped with Ashton. What was the point in all of this? He was just going to tell me to stay strong and be on my merry way.

"I wanted to talk about this in the car but," he shook his head, "but here we are. So I'm leaving the choice to you." He reached inside his leather jacket and pulled out three white envelopes.

"What choice?" I was holding back tears that I knew would come out if he told me that I was a rolling stone.

"These are your last three paychecks from Roth. You can take these, and Hannah will set you up in a place far from the city. Or, you can stay here-and work for me." Donovan's voice was softer than usual but still held the firm tone of a businessman with an offer on the table.

But regardless of his tone, I was in awe as I studied the envelopes and Donovan's face. I had to process this, at the nth hour which was a surprised because I never received choices or options. I barely had agency in my life so I should have been leaping for joy at Donovan's proposal. But I wasn't. Because what he'd presented were two extreme options that a week ago would've ushered a different reaction from me. But today, despite my earlier anxiety, I knew what I wanted. Or at least, I had to pretend that I knew. Because what I wanted and what I knew was best for me would evidently make the outcome of all of this very difficult.

"Is this really my choice?" I asked rather timidly but watched as Donovan gave a short nod.

"Of course it is."

I inhaled deeply and then let the breath out gently so that my voice would stay steady. I was scared of my own response but he'd said it was truly my choice and therefore I had to stand by it. I was now free from Charlotte, Lush, and Greene as if I could start a new. That newness didn't consist of crime and cold intentions.

"I can't do-whatever it is that you do." I said, looking up at Donovan.

Donovan's eyes said that he knew exactly what I meant and they slowly cast downward before returning to me as he straightened up. "C'mon." He ushered me toward the black car that Hannah was inside of.

Donovan handed the envelopes to me with slight hesitation. I kept my focus on him as if he would suddenly present a third option for me to consider. One that would allow me to stay with him, protected from the Ashton's and Greene's of the world. But that option wasn't available for a man whose life revolved around crime and the capacity in which someone could accept criminal activity. I wasn't that someone.

So I took the envelopes from his hand, quickly turning my back to him so that I could get into the car.

"Rosemary," he called before I stepped a foot into the backseat. I peered over my shoulder, "you're a smart girl, don't get stuck at another Lush." It was almost a warning, but for my own good. One that was laced with care and concern. He didn't have to explicitly say that I wouldn't see him again after today. Saying this was more than enough because I had a second chance at life and I didn't want to screw it up.

I responded with a tight smile then joined Hannah inside the car. My throat was tight and my stomach fluttered at the reality of my situation. I'd always been alone, but Donovan had been the first person to challenge that aspect of my life. It would be difficult to return to my independence after the experience I had. Sure it was bitter sweet, but ultimately it had to happen this way.

"Donovan picked out a great place in Riverdale for you." Hannah said, crossing her bare legs at the ankle.

I cocked a brow, "so he knew what my decision would be?"

"I think he knew what the right decision was-for you." Hannah smiled at me as the car pulled away from the Upper East Side place where I had felt at home.

"You've had to go through a lot Rosemary." She touched my hand. "But you're still pure. We all knew it from the beginning."

I didn't know how to respond to her. I'd never been told that I was pure. Lush girls, whores, shot girls, none of us were considered pure. And yet, sitting beside someone who had once been called all of those names, gave me hope that I could still be seen in a wholesome light.

Maybe it was high time I repeated three new words to myself since I no longer was and would never be a Lush girl again. I owed it to myself and to Donovan. I was Independent, Safe, and Pure and I had the most unlikely people to thank for it.

So without a second thought, I glanced back at the distant figure that was Donovan and whispered a soft, "Thank you."

Epilogue

1.5 Years Later

This will be the most monumental moment in my life.

Well, second place to getting kidnapped.

Or maybe third place because I'd been kidnapped twice.

Actually, a solid fourth place since leaving Donovan to live alone in my comfortable Riverdale apartment for the past year and a half was definitely high on the list.

Living alone had been "monumental" because there was no room for me to back peddle in life even if the first few months had been rough. Visits from Hannah hadn't helped fill the pit in my stomach from Donovan's absense. However, when I was five months in to living alone I was finally able to find that closure and fill that pit by stepping outside and doing things I enjoyed. Those pleasures had helped me find Grant. Actually, Grant had found me, and cared for me, and loved me.

So yes, this occasion would place fourth on my list, I thought and sighed as I peered out the window where the Greek revival style mansion rolled into my line of sight. The long white pillars, elaborate greenery, and grand front porch adorned elegant decor in honor of the special day. A large "Congratulations Newlyweds" banner hung high at the front of the house.

The white Rolls Royce that I rode inside of pulled up behind six other identical vehicles in the circular driveway. There were no other guests in front. Was I late? I checked the time on my screen and as if on cue, Grant's name appeared.

"This is where I leave you." The driver said. I looked up from my phone screen and saw him smile at me through the rear view mirror.

"Thank you." I silenced the call, grabbed the pink gift box, and scooted our of the backseat to head inside of the house.

The faint sound of classical music filled the hallway and helped lead me to the backyard where the gift was taken from me and I was escorted to the semi-circle of white chairs around an arch made of peach colored drapery and peonies. The backyard was something out of Town & Country and I almost wondered how dirty money could afford such a delicate and thoughtful livelihood. It was charming.

"Rosemary!" I heard a high pitched voice call.

I looked around at the hundreds of faces that surrounded me, but easily identified the caller as Grace who waved her arms above her head. I slid down the row and settled in beside her.

"They have a beautiful home." I said, giving the grounds another scan.

"You should see the entire interior. Ten bedrooms, six bathrooms, a sauna, and I swear there's a bowling alley in the basement." Grace brushed a piece of lint off of her royal blue dress.

A year ago I would have never considered spending any amount of time with Grace. After all, she had stated that she wanted nothing to do with anyone involved with Donovan after Ashton got a hold of her and even before that we had never bonded in any way.

But life had an odd way of turning tables and after seeing Grace casually one morning, we'd connected and eventually befriended one another. Hannah found herself in the same position after she noticed how often Grace stopped by my apartment.

My phone screen illuminated with Grant's name again but this time Grace stopped me from silencing it as if this was the proper setting to answer a phone call.

"Oh, you're getting some tonight." She winked. "You should've brought him, the house is big enough to have some fun without getting caught."

I gave Grace a twisted expression and chuckled at her humor. Before I could respond, the organ began to play Wagner's Lohengrin to signal the beginning of the procession as male and female pairs walked down the isle in gray suits and dresses, respectively, with peach accents.

Time seemed to stop however when I noticed Donovan gliding slowly down the isle in his well tailored gray suit and his perfectly coiffed blonde combover. His facial hair was lower than I had remembered but allowed for his usual bold features to soften.

I tried to follow his movements down the isle but eventually my focus was blocked as everyone stood and Hannah appeared in her sheath style white dress, with a bouquet clutched in her hands, and her beautiful face covered by a white veil. She stood across from Nate once her father brought her to the arch. Nate's eyes were tenderly and admirably staring at his soon-to-be wife.

Before the two said "I do" Nate turned to retrieve the ring from Donovan, who gave his back a pat and handed it over.

I hadn't seen Donovan in more than a year and I'd prepared for this day. For the day I would see Donovan again in a non captive capacity. But I was still stunned at the sight as if his position as best man had come out of the blue. After all, Donovan was technically the reason I was at this wedding in the first place.

Regardless, when the ceremony was over, my heart sped in anticipation of cocktail hour where mingling was mandatory. I rushed to grab a glass of rosé in order to calm myself from the anxious feeling I was getting knowing that Donovan still existed and could be anywhere in the crowd.

"Do you still fuck Donovan?" I asked Grace without hesitation.

Grace gaped at my question and furrowed her brows in confusion.

"What?! Rose, I'm engaged!" She wiggled her fingers near my face as a reminder. I'd forgotten our bond began when I realized that she was over Donovan since she'd met a man that worked in the government sector.

"Oh-yeah." My mind was clouded as I surveyed my surroundings.

"You seem distracted." Grace noticed while shaking her head. "I'll get you some hard liquor." I nodded as Grace walked toward the outdoor bar.

The fountain nearby looked refreashing and I was tempted to use the water to splash my face because my body was at the same temperature barometer as a bonfire.

I needed to calm down, this was exactly what I hadn't wanted which was why I'd chosen to be on my own. I needed to grow without relying on others and without feeling as if everyone around me could control my choices. So why was I so anxious?

I sighed deeply and walked inside the house to search for a bathroom to freshen up but found myself right beside Hannah who was smiling for a few pictures.

"Congratulations." I tapped her shoulder. She turned away from her family and beamed when she noticed that it had been my voice.

"Rosemary! My true maid of honor." She only slightly joked since she had been obligated to choose her family to fill her bridesmaids positions. Something about family tradition but it didn't devalue our close friendship.

"Everything was so beautiful and I'm so happy for you."

"Nate!" Hannah called out to her husband who came over with a glass of scotch in hand.

I'd assumed that he didn't care to see me since he hadn't in the past so when he smiled and touched my arm I was caught off guard.

"It's great to see you Rosemary."

"Really?" I cocked my head to the side.

Hannah and Nate both laughed as if I were joking but the question was an honest one. Nate had never liked me and although I'd seen Hannah almost weekly for the past year and a half, I'd only seen Nate once from my bedroom window when he was parked out front to pick up Hannah for some wedding planning business.

"You're so funny." Hannah embraced me then her name sounded from across the hallway. She grimaced and took Nate's hand. "It's my uncle. Rose, please save me after the reception so that we can dance together and take pictures."

"I'll be sure to steal you from everyone else." I assured her as she smirked playfully and then dismissed herself at the behest of her family.

It was inspiring to see the two of them and I couldn't believe that Hannah was the embodiment of a Lush girl gone wife. It was considered a myth back when Lush was around and I'd been convinced. I hadn't told Grant about my past at Lush but Hannah had told me it wasn't worth mentioning. Especially, since I'd told him about Donovan and that came with a slew of questions I hadn't been prepared to answer. Not in the beginning of our relation-

"Would you believe me if I said it's great to see you?" A familiar voice said close to my ear as I reached for a passing glass of wine.

I didn't need to turn around yet to identify the speaker. I took a moment to relish the confident and soothing tone that I hadn't heard in a long time. The same voice that evoked a plethora of emotions while still easing my nerves.

I spun around slowly and faced him. He looked amused, tilting his glass to his lips as his eyes focused on me with intensity. It was by far one of the most intimidating expressions but I'd missed it because it was distinct to Donovan. It's not that I'd forgotten how handsome he was, it's that I'd forgotten how his glare made me stir and his smirk kept me wondering.

I parted my lips because I wanted to say something that made sense. I'd practiced for this moment. But I said the first thing that my brain and tongue could muster up.

"Donovan, I uh-didn't think I would see you here."

He cocked an eyebrow and my face flushed with embarrassment. Wow. As soon as I'd said the sentence I wanted to hit my head against a wall. Of course he would be here. It wasn't like I was at some random co workers baby shower. It was his right hands wedding!

"Well, I did but-I didn't think we would have a conversation or speak to each other at all or-or uh-" Rosemary, get it together. I told myself. I hadn't seen him in more than a year and this was my conversation starter? He'd kept it short and simple while I stood dumbly trying to recite a speech.

So I exhaled deeply, gathered my thoughts, and finally said, "How're you Donovan?" I looked right into his eyes. I was different and I had to show it by curbing my nerves in his presence.

"I'm good." He leaned his arm on the banister of the grand staircase. "How're you?"

"Busy. I'm still in the apartment you helped me with. I mean, my lease is up next month but I'm in the process of finding something new."

"And I'm assuming you're working now since you stopped accepting any help." Donovan mentioned with a smirk.

He'd paid my rent for the first few months while I looked for a job and Hannah would sometimes come around with a few extra hands to restock my kitchen. Eventually, I notified Hannah that I didn't want assistance anymore and she evidently relayed the message to Donovan since she relayed all of my correspondence to him.

"Yeah, but don't worry, it's not a Lush type of job." Donovan chuckled.

"I wasn't worried at all." He said. I caught his stare again then blinked up at him.

"You weren't worried about me?"

"I was-at first. Then I remembered that you survived a week with me and a dog you were terrified of." I felt my lips curl into a smile at the memory as I sipped the rosé.

"You make it sound trivial."

"Your fear of Stone was trivial. Your fear of me was-cute now that I think about it." He shrugged while glaring down at me.

For the first time in a long time, I realized that I missed the soft glint that reassured me in anxious situations. It was specific to Donovan and it might've been because the softness was juxtaposed with his dominant stature. But whatever the reason, I could stare at him for hours and listen to him for days.

"My fear of you still exists." I pushed some hair behind my ear. "Just for different reasons." My eyes moved to the front of his pants without my permission before returning to his eyes.

There was something about the way he glared that brought me back to the day we fucked. I thought about it occasionally but at this very moment images of that particular night flashed in my mind. I wanted him, again, even if it was just one last time. So without a second thought, I took a slow sip of wine then licked my glossed lips delicately, biting down on the bottom.

He focused on my simple seductive gesture then switched his focus upward to the staircase. He was distracted and for a moment I'd thought that my attempt had been in vain which would have been more embarrassing than my stutter session earlier.

However, Donovan placed his drink down on a table then touched my lower back.

"C'mon." He led me up the steps, past a few wedding guests who were consumed in conversation.

No one paid attention to us as we walked up and a slight part of me felt bad for leaving the wedding even if it was for a few minutes. Maybe Donovan wanted to tell me he'd gotten engaged or maybe he needed privacy to tell me how everything with Ashton turned out.

But all of my speculation was put to rest when Donovan placed his hands on my waist and pushed me against the lily white wall of the hallway. His hand moved up my body and tangled into my hair, giving it a tug before placing a kiss on my neck. My gasp was loud but only loud enough to be heard through the hallway.

"I missed you." I admitted, wanting him to desperately devour me right here, right now. I wanted him. Every part of him.

Donovan pulled harder and pressed his body to mine letting the sexual energy between us charge up our cores.

I felt a soft vibration and at first I thought Donovan had come prepared with toys. I was all too familiar with a mobile vibrator since I had one in my purse at home. However, the vibration was deceiving as I glanced down and realized shortly that it was my cell phone. The rectangular screen illuminated in my hand.

"Grant?" Donovan asked. I sighed.

"He's-he's my-" Donovan didn't wait for me to finish. He took my phone and tossed it aside on the ground. Then he pressed his lips to mine for the first time in a long time.

His physical touch awoke the lust filled urge inside of me that hadn't been satisfied in months. It was exciting, even as he pushed my body back into a room and switched the light on, all the while keeping his lips pressed to mine and his arms tight around my body.

"I need to be inside you." His husky voice said close to my ear, causing a shiver down my spine. "Tell me that's what you want Rose." He removed his suspenders from his shoulders.

"I want you inside me." I said through fast breaths as my heart sped. Donovan lifted me onto the marble bathroom counter. I pulled him closer to my body, allowing him to slid his smooth hands up so that my dress would follow.

"I missed you too baby." He finally said but I couldn't react properly to his words because in an instant, I felt him insert himself into my dripping pussy.

I grabbed at him for stability, knowing that this wouldn't last long for me because I couldn't contain my level of sexual ecstasy. So I wrapped my arms around his neck and held tight as he stroked in and out of my tight hole, squeezing my thighs as I moaned into his ears.

"Don-Donovan." I gasped, throwing my head back. Donovan clamped his hand over my mouth to suppress my loud sounds but quickened his pace in order to take me over the edge.

I missed the full feeling he'd given me the first time we had sex. His strong arms were firm on my body, his soft lips were caressing my skin, and his incredible dick kept my pussy wet and satisfied. It was unlike any experience I'd ever had sexually and I felt myself loosing control.

Donovan grabbed me in his arms and lifted me off of the counter so that he could fuck me against the door. I can't help it, I thought as I weaved my fingers through his blonde hair and breathed my final words.

"I'm cumming, I'm cumming Don-I'm-" I tightened my grip.

"Cum on it." He demanded as I released right in that moment.

Donovan grunted then pulled out, still holding me up with one arm as his other reached down and he too reached his climax. • • • • • •It took a couple minutes for us to come down from the high and maybe ten more minutes for us to look presentable enough to face the public. But by now the reception had probably started which meant Donovan was expected to appear and do his best man speech.

"I forgot how amazing you feel." Donovan said as he leaned back on the counter and watched me run my fingers through my hair in an effort to return it to its laid state.

"So I guess we both needed that." I smiled at his reflection in the mirror. He chuckled, took my hand to bring me toward him and kissed my forehead.

"How do I look?"

I scanned his frame and shrugged, "Good not great." I joked. He actually looked better than great as if he hadn't just fucked my brains out.

"Well," Donovan opened the bathroom door for me, "It'll have to do since I have a speech to give. Let's head down."

I walked through the door, a bit disappointed at the reality that I'd once again teased myself into thinking this would last at all. I wanted to be honest with myself and with what I wanted but I needed to be honest with Donovan too.

Before we reached the bottom of the grand stairs, I turned to stop him behind me by placing my hand on his chest.

"Donovan, I have to be honest with you before we go another year without seeing each other."

"Honest? About what?." He gave a confused expression as I inhaled deep.

"I really am doing well on my own."

"I know, I wouldn't expect anything less."

"No, just listen." My heart was racing as I tried to get my thoughts together. "I miss you and I know we just released a lot of-of um tension, but I want to be around you."

"You're losing me Rosemary."

"Sorry, I'm saying I want to be around you but it's not about what we just did. Honestly, it's not even about the apartment. It's the fact that when I met you I was so scared and I could barely speak up. But you did something to help me and I-I just love-" Both Donovan and I sighed at the same time.

"Don't say it." He shook his head. "You made a mistake tonight. Don't make another one."

"A mistake? Why would you say that?" Just as I asked, my phone began to vibrate and Grant's name appeared on the screen. Again.

Donovan followed my gaze to the screen. "Oh." I cursed under my breath.

"Yeah." He nodded his head. "Enjoy the reception Rose." Donovan started down the stairs again.

"No, Donovan!" I touched his arm to stop him. "It's not what you think. At all." I let out a short laugh.

"What do I think?"

"You think I just cheated because you think Grant's my boyfriend. Or my fiancé. Or whatever." I laughed. Donovan came close in front of me without the same amusement and studied my face.

"So who is he?"

"Grant is-my ex." He cocked an eyebrow at me in disbelief.

"He's calling you. Repeatedly."

"Well, it's a long story." I sighed. It definitely looked bad that I had ultimately racked up fifteen missed calls from one person. "The break up happened a month ago. He's not over it." The breakup had been civil but I hadn't shared the news with anyone. Grant knew about Donovan for the most part and since he was supposed to be my plus one, he was aware that Donovan would be present. So he was calling as a sick method of controlling my association.

I looked up at Donovan whose lips finally curled up in a smirk as he touched my chin.

"You need me to handle this guy?"

"If 'handle' means shoot him in the foot, then no ." I smiled, oddly turned on by his question.

Donovan chuckled and shook his head. "'Handle' means straighten him out."

"That's not necessary." I assured him. "But I love you for offering." I casually admitted.

"Oh, you love me now?" He took my hand.

"Don't tease me about it." I pulled from his grip and gave him a playful nudge. "I love being around you like after the Ashton situation. We should-go back to that."

Donovan stared at me for a moment to gauge how serious my comment was. "I'll pick you up tomorrow at six for dinner." I nodded in reply. "And I'll have Hannah call some people to help you move your stuff out of the apartment. In the mean time you'll stay with me until you find a new place."

"I would like that."

Donovan didn't have to say much else for the both of us to know what it all meant. I wanted to be in his life and I didn't want to feel that emptiness of being without him again. Though it wasn't the end all of my existence, it just felt so right being near him now. Simply extending the offer for me to stay with him was hopeful in what our relationship could be.

"So you're okay with my business now?" His question brought me back to the day he'd given me a choice that would decide my future.

He was worried but I'd thought about this before and over the past year. I reached up to smooth his suit jacket then patted his chest.

"Are you asking that question because you want to protect me again?"

"I feel inclined to always protect you." He kissed the hand that was closest to his face. "Get use to it."

"In that case, I trust you with your business and with having me in your life. You'll keep me safe." I winked at him.

Donovan slowly nodded and welcomed the kiss I placed on his lips before he touched my waist.

"C'mon, I don't need Hannah pressing me about you disappearing for the third time since she's known you."

We both laughed as we descended the stairs to the illuminated backyard where the reception was soon to begin under the soft glow of the sunset sky.

A sunset sky marked a new beginning. One that displayed my independence. One that allowed the past to stay in the past. And most importantly, one that included Donovan Faust in my life.

CPSIA information can be obtained
at www.ICGtesting.com
Printed in the USA
BVHW031438091222
653840BV00009B/741

9 781837 612659